The Survivors

The
Survivors

Gregory Janicke

Marshall Cavendish

Marshall Cavendish Corporation
99 White Plains Road
Tarrytown, NY 10591
www.marshallcavendish.us/kids

Library of Congress Cataloging-in-Publication Data
Janicke, Gregory.
 [Attack of the Shadow Beasts]
 The Survivors / by Gregory Janicke. — 1st Marshall Cavendish pbk. ed.
     p. cm. — (Outcasts ; bk. 2)
 "Originally published in Malaysia [under title, "Attack of the Shadow
Beasts"] by Times Editions - Marshall Cavendish, 2004"—Copyright p.
  Summary: As they struggle to hold onto the hope of finding HayVen, the
Outcasts, a group of teenagers struggling to survive in a world of chaos,
encounter new friends and old enemies while hiding in the Font of Knowledge,
and are attacked by the Shadow Beasts.
  ISBN-13: 978-0-7614-5365-9
  ISBN-10: 0-7614-5365-2
  ISBN-10: 9833318649 (Malaysian ed.)
 [1. Survival—Fiction. 2. Fantasy.] I. Title. II. Series.
 PZ7.J2428Sur 2007
 [Fic]—dc22
 2006053065

The text of this book is set in Adobe Garamond.
Printed in Malaysia
First North American edition
10 9 8 7 6 5 4 3 2 1

ITC Marshall Cavendish

To Yasmina Joy

❖ ❖ ❖

Chapter 1

Marina knelt by the edge of the underground stream. A face gazed up at her.

The face reflected in the still, silver water looked familiar — the same blue-green skin color as hers, same dark eyes and long black hair. The same large, pointed ears that the children laughed at every day.

The face was hers, but she looked old and tired. Her cheeks were sunken. She hadn't eaten much lately, giving most of her rations to the children at each meal.

There were forty-five of them in the group, thirteen of whom were small children who shouted, cried, laughed, danced and sang. They seemed to be all emotion and no sense.

They called themselves Outcasts. Each member of the group had somehow survived the attacking Antibodies. The Antibodies were tall, swift and brutal. Their skin were transparent — in bright light, Marina had seen their throbbing muscles, twisting bones and cold, black hearts. They moved with lightning speed and the deadliest precision. They had attacked Marina's Quae Community, carrying off her family, burning the homes, destroying all memory of their joyous life by the sea.

Gyro, the leader of the Outcasts, had saved her. She, in turn, helped him rescue other young people throughout the land who had survived Antibody attacks. Together the Outcasts searched for HayVen, a place of peace.

Marina was a scout, a leader. She not only had to find food, water and safe shelter for everyone, but also felt compelled to find a purpose and direction. The Outcasts were elsewhere in the maze of caves she now explored, safe for the moment. She knew it was foolish to think they would be safe for long.

Marina slowly stood. She thought she saw a face other than hers in the water, but it vanished.

I need rest. And food.

And Jax ...

Marina stiffened. Why had a thought of Jax come to mind? He was her fellow scout, but he had a big, round, pink head and huge eyes. He looked as if he were constantly choking. Every time she wanted to act, to move, to run, he wanted to stop, think and discuss. He didn't understand that the fine art of scouting required instinct and precise action. Discussions were best left at the campfire.

Still, he had proven himself in the attack of the Shadow Beasts. He had crawled under the very feet of Antibodies. The newest Outcast, a cunning character named Dav'yn, had actually shot an arrow into Jax's shoulder, but her round-headed friend endured.

Marina looked at her reflection one last time. Without hesitating, she dove into the crystal-clear water. At first, it was a shock to her skin. The water was bitterly cold. It didn't matter, though. She had grown up by the sea. Her father had taught her how to swim when she was a baby. By now, she was an expert.

If Father could see me now, Marina thought. She felt the grip of sadness as she swam. *If only I could see him now ... and my home ... my friends ...*

Marina swam onward. Unlike the foamy, roiling sea of her homeland, this river was calm, smooth as glass. She swam underwater for as long as she could, then broke the surface. She smiled. Her skin glistened and her long, black ponytail rested like a wet rope on her back. Nothing felt better than water.

She dove underwater again. She opened her eyes. Marina saw jutting reefs and bright pink coral. Below, luminous orange fish were huddled head-to-head, looking like the spokes of a large wheel. A school of rainbow fish the size of her hand wriggled past her without fear.

She grabbed a sunken reef and pulled on it to propel herself forward. She swam through coral that reached for her like long green fingers. A round, pink fish with searching brown eyes drifted past her.

A Jax fish! she thought with amusement.

If only she didn't have to come up for air! The more Marina saw below the surface, the more she wanted to explore. Fish with yellow and red stripes appeared. A purple starfish tumbled like a child. An iridescent stingray scuttled across the bottom of the river.

Marina rose to the surface. *What is this place?* she wondered. She would have expected such sights off the shore of her homeland but not here in the depths of the earth.

What magic is this?

A white wafer with tiny spines puffed open and shut in the water. Marina guessed that she'd better not touch it. It might have been a poisonous jellyfish.

She could hear Jax telling her right now, "Don't go near that thing!" He worried all the time. Her father had told her that she never worried enough — she always jumped before looking.

Marina floated on her back. Although the underground light wasn't as bright here as it was back at the camp, it still revealed the towering walls of crystal. They appeared to go up forever, like a magic mountain. The glassy formations seemed to drink light from the heavens and cast rainbows at dazzling angles in the underground realm.

She thought she saw two tiny chips of green light, but they vanished.

There was a soft noise, like a rock dropped in water.

Marina kept swimming.

Part of her simply wanted to explore the unknown. Another part of her wanted to get away from the Outcasts and their bickering and endless tumble of problems. They had come from many communities, many cultures. They spoke different languages; they had wildly different customs. They didn't always agree on things. In fact, Marina couldn't remember a time when they all agreed on the same subject. There was always argument and complaint. There was hunger. There was exhaustion. There was the fear that, at any moment, Antibodies would strike.

Here in the water, there was peace. It was like being home again for her.

Home.

She would never see her home again. The thought constantly haunted her. Each night before falling asleep, Marina would imagine her sturdy wooden home built along the seashore in the Quae Community. In her memory she saw her mother, father and two older brothers — hauling goods from ship to port, sharpening harpoons and mending sails. She pictured the rock from which she dove into the sea each day. She could almost feel the sea breeze in her face, could almost hear the keening of gulls.

Gone forever …

Enough. She needed to concentrate on matters at hand. She wondered what Jax would make of the bright coral, colorful fish and crystal walls. He never had immediate answers for anything, but he never gave up until he answered a question or solved a problem. She had grown to like his big, pink head and huge, gaping eyes. He would lean and stare as if gazing right through an object. Unlike the others, he could actually see in the dark.

Marina shuddered.

I have to stop thinking about Jax!

Jax wasted too much of his time pining over Lynai'seth of the Shi'vaal Community. Lynai'seth spoke in high tones, giving her an air of mystery, like a haunting song. Unlike Marina's scratched and scarred body, Lynai'seth had perfect purple skin and long golden hair. She had an ability to calm the children with her soothing voice, but sometimes she acted with a haughty reserve as if she were queen and everyone else her servants.

Marina wondered if she should tell Jax what she knew about Lynai'seth and the people of her Shi'vaal Community. There was a reason why he and Lynai'seth could never be a couple …

Her ears twitched.

Something was in the water, just ahead of her.

I'm on it, she said to herself.

She dipped below the water, swimming past blood-red fish that were only mildly interested in her. She looked ahead and saw something like a gray fin curl deep into the water.

She came up for air. Marina knew it was foolish to keep following whatever it was she had seen. The road had been a long and hard one for the Outcasts. Her recent fight with the Antibodies had left her battered and exhausted. She should have been resting back at the campsite with the others.

She was Marina of the Quae Community, though, daughter of Fontana and Azur, sister of Isthen and Mer. For her, the recollection of her proud lineage was enough to send her back down into the water.

She could almost hear her father grinding his teeth at her for being so impetuous.

The fin, or whatever it was, moved ahead of her.

Each time she came up for air, the world grew a little darker. The crystal face of the walls now seemed smudged with black rock.

Something rose in a gray bubble, bobbed for a moment, then dipped back into the water. Marina was sure she had seen a pair of green eyes. Maybe this was yet another type of fish she had never seen before, one that would not only serve her appetite but also several of the children back at camp.

She slid her hand along the knife strapped to her thigh.

Time to go fishing.

She took a deep breath and dove underwater. This time she had purpose and direction. She flutter kicked.

There —

She saw twin green eyes but only a faint outline of a body. The fish seemed translucent, a milky blob constantly changing its shape.

It —

She saw another pair of green eyes. Two of them must have been swimming together.

More food for the children.

She was about to break the surface for another breath of air. The fish doubled back. Before she could grab her knife, it rammed into her and slipped away.

It returned and circled. Marina kicked. She managed to tug her knife from its sheath. As the fish lunged again, she jammed the knife into it.

An unholy shriek tore through the water. Marina used the moment to head for the surface.

She could see light coming through the water. She was an arm's length from air.

Just as the top of her head broke the surface, something coiled around her leg and tugged her downward. She couldn't see what was wrapped around her. It felt like a tentacle. The tentacle excreted something that burned her bare leg.

She plunged the knife into the creature again. A milky substance oozed from the wound.

The creature coiled another tentacle around her.

Then she saw it.

The creature had the texture and tentacles of a giant jellyfish. Its poison burned her legs. Its strength held her underwater.

The two pairs of green eyes came into focus.

The creature was a shifting, writhing, murderous mass.

With two human faces.

Marina felt something impossible — a crushing pressure in her chest and neck.

She was drowning.

It was a sensation she had never known. It was a sensation no one in the Quae Community had ever known until the horrid invasion of Antibodies.

Drowning —

The two human faces pressed down on her. They seemed to be — smiling.

Marina gasped. The final bubbles rose from her mouth. She felt water fill her lungs.

Her body went limp. She no longer felt the grip of the creature, the horrid burning sensation on her legs.

She felt nothing.

She saw nothing.

Darkness.

Chapter 2

Then there was faint pink and gray light, like soft sunrise.

If this was the Realm Beyond HayVen, it was warm. There was a sweet scent and even sweeter taste.

Then a sudden, violent, wrenching pain. Water releasing from the lungs. Coughing, choking. More pain. Gasping.

Then the sweet scent and sweeter taste. Bright pink light. Something sweet touched her lips. Something delicious.

Some — one?

Someone was …

Someone was kissing her!

Whether this was a dream, After Life or real, Marina would not allow this! She made a fist and swung it with all her might. Her fist struck her assailant's face like a rock.

"Eeeyah!"

The assailant fell away from her. Marina drew quick breaths, spat water and rolled to her knees.

The assailant reeled with pain.

"Fiend!" Marina cried. She pounced on her attacker and hit him again. He weakly defended himself, covering his face with his arms.

"Marina …" the assailant gasped.

She looked at him. "Jax?"

Jax slowly turned to her. His nose and mouth were bleeding. He cupped his hands over his eyes.

"Jax?"

"You were — then I …" his voice trailed off.

"You were kissing me!"

"I was … saving you."

"You call that a rescue?"

Jax wiped blood from his face. "You were … away from camp too long. I followed you."

Marina sat back. Her legs burned from the attack in the water. "No one can follow my trail."

"I saw —"

"Saw what?"

"You were swimming. Then you sank."

"It's called diving underwater."

"I climbed along the edge of the river. You didn't come up. This — arm came up out of the water. Two arms. Three. I stuck my knife in it."

Marina carefully touched her legs. The pain deepened. "So did I."

"The — thing — cried out," Jax said. "Went away. You didn't come up, so I jumped in the water to find you."

"You can't swim."

Jax spat blood. "Didn't matter."

"So you pulled me out of the water and started kissing me? Freak!"

"It's called — revival. No. Resuscitation."

"It's called sick."

"Terra told me about it. You get the water out and breathe air in."

Marina flinched. "You BREATHED in me?"

"You looked dead."

"You could have asked first."

"You were dead."

"That's no excuse. In my community, we live by the Quae Credo — the Rules of Life. A woman and man find signs that they belong together. Then they stand side-by-side at the Ripening Ceremony. They don't touch closely until the Binding. Then they're bound for life."

"If I recall, you kept hugging me when we fought Antibodies. Three times. I counted."

"That was different! That was the way someone hugs a lost pet. The way Klanga hugs Feelie. You kissed and breathed in me. That was — wrong."

"I'll remember that the next time I save you."

"You didn't save me! No boy saves me!"

"You're right, Marina. I waited until you were nearly dead for the chance to kiss you. There. It's over for life. Can we go back to camp now? I'm bleeding and my eyes hurt."

"Too much staring at me in the dark."

"You hit me."

"I ..." Marina looked at Jax. "You surprised me."

"Marina, you always surprise me."

Marina's skin tingled when Jax said her name that way. "We should go."

She tried to stand, but her skin burned. Her muscles ached. Her bones felt like dust. She fell.

Marina saw a filmy mass along the shin of her right leg. It had the same color and texture as the creature that had poisoned her.

"All right, let's go," Jax said, still on the ground.

"Can't you see what's happened to me? My legs?"

Jax took a deep breath and released. "I can't see anything at the moment."

"You're always so dramatic."

Jax slowly turned his head towards her. His left eye was a thin slit. The right eye — the one she had struck — was black and swollen shut.

"No, Marina, I'm not. I'm blind."

"You can't see a thing?"

"No."

"Then I've got to get you back to camp. Terra can work some of her healing magic. Maybe she'll breathe on you."

"Maybe," Jax said. He rose and took a few steps.

"Stop!" Marina cried.

"Why?"

"You're going to fall into the river. And — I can't stand up."

"So?"

"So … I need your help."

"Oh, no! If I help you, you'll hit me again."

"I vow on my family."

Jax paused. He turned towards her, stumbled, then extended his hand. They took two steps together and fell.

"That went well," Jax said.

"We need to be — closer."

Jax stood, helped Marina to her feet and slid his arm around her waist. Marina put her arm around his shoulders. They tightened their hold on each other.

"This is a violation of at least twenty-four rules of the Quae Credo," Marina said.

Jax helped her walk along the slick rocks. "Maybe it means you and I are bound for life."

"In your dreams."

They moved cautiously along the river for a while. The caverns breathed their foul winds.

It was hard for Marina to be upset with Jax, especially during treacherous times like these. He was always trying to be helpful. She looked at her fellow scout and took pity. "Jax," she said, "I didn't know."

"Didn't know what?"

"That you were … you."

Jax smiled faintly. "I'll take that as an apology."

"What is an 'apology?'"

"It's when people seek forgiveness. In my community, forgiveness and mercy are everything. *Were* everything. My community is gone for good."

"But there's — HayVen. Like Gyro says."

"You don't believe him."

"Are you a wizard? Can you read my mind, Jax?"

"I watch you. I am — I was good at seeing things. And I listen to the way you say things. I don't always understand your language, but I want to understand your meaning."

Marina considered this statement. For some unknown reason, she liked knowing that Jax listened to her.

She liked walking arm-in-arm with him. As she thought about the moments before she hit him in the face, she realized that she liked kissing him. For those few sweet moments, life felt perfect.

Are there exceptions to the Credo of my community? she

wondered. She didn't remember any rules about bright pink Kertan boys helping her escape underground terrors …

It didn't matter. She had blinded him. She doubted he would ever kiss her again.

Fine. I am a warrior. A scout. Jax and I —

"*Rindu vyn ftoss Quae,*" she muttered in a classical dialect of her community.

"What?" Jax asked. "What did you say?"

Never in this life, she thought. "It means, 'Keep going.'"

"No — wait."

"What?"

"Something's coming."

There was a pause. A rumbling. A sick, oozing sound, like the opening of a creature's mouth, the cold twisting of its sinew as it readied itself to attack.

The damp air burst with hideous shrieking. Rocks fell. Crystal shattered and rained in shards.

"MARINA!"

Marina felt Jax slip from her arms. Her legs gave out from under her.

She saw the creature from the water.

It was now on land.

It was not alone.

Chapter 3

"What's happening?" Jax cried. "Marina!"

Marina rolled onto her stomach and used her arms to creep toward Jax. "Creatures," she said.

"Shadow Beasts? Antibodies?"

Marina saw that Jax carried a knife. She pulled it from the sheath. "No. Something else."

"What do they look like?"

"Not now, Jax."

"I can't help you if I don't know what they look like."

"I count six of them," Marina said. "Maybe more in the shadows. You can see through them like Antibodies, but they don't have arms or legs. Tentacles. They keep changing size and shape. And, Jax — they have *faces*."

"What do you mean?"

"Each creature has two faces in it. The faces slide up and down inside the bodies."

"I'm better off not seeing these things. Marina, what do you want me to do?"

"Wait."

"For what?"

"My signal."

"What signal? It's not like you can climb somewhere and jump them by surprise."

"I can crawl. I can still protect you."

"Protect me? What about you?"

The creatures twisted, slithered, drew near them. Then they

screamed. Their shrill voices cracked the crystal walls. Crystal pieces dropped like darts on the ground and into the stream.

"AHH!"

A blade of glass struck Jax in the shoulder. Marina quickly reached over and pulled it out. Jax was bleeding.

"We've got to get out of here!" she cried.

"How?"

Marina forced herself on all fours. The pain tearing through her legs was unbearable. She clenched her teeth and tried standing. Her legs felt on fire. "I — am Marina of the Quae Community," she said through her teeth, "daughter of Fontana and Azur, sister of Isthen and Mer." She knelt. She slowly brought her left leg forward and placed her left forearm on it like a steel lever. "I am Marina …" she said, the pain bringing tears to her eyes. She locked her right hand on her left wrist. "… of the Quae Community." She slowly rose, muscles taut, heart pounding, eyes blind with tears.

"I — AM — MARINA!"

She stood.

The creatures paused.

Her name echoed through the cave, sliding off into darkness.

Jax raised an arm helplessly. "Marina!"

"I'm on it, Jax," she said.

She took a small step and nearly fell. She rested her hands on her legs and caught her breath. She would not fall. Not now.

"Give me your hand."

Jax reached up to her. Marina grabbed his arm and lifted him to his feet. "Can you see yet?" she asked.

"No. What's our plan?"

"I carry you out of here and stab creatures along the way."

"That's a plan?"

"Do you have a better idea?"

"Can we go backwards?"

Marina looked over her shoulder. "No. More creatures."

"What about in the river?"

Three creatures with their horrid, sliding faces broke the surface of the stream. Their tentacles curled like hundreds of black snakes toward them.

"The river is a bad idea."

"So we're surrounded by poisonous, two-faced blobs."

"Jax, you have a firm grasp of the obvious."

"Let me go, Marina. I'll be the bait. You run."

"You call that a plan? I can barely walk."

"Wait," Jax said. "Wait." He pressed his fingers to his head and leaned forward. Marina hated this pose. It meant Jax was thinking.

"Not now!" she said.

"Wait."

Marina waited. She looked behind her, then left and right. The creatures seemed to be forming a giant wall, their hideous eyes bulging, swimming, rolling inside their bodies.

Finally, Jax spoke in a whisper. "Marina, why haven't they attacked us yet?"

"They're …" She lowered her voice, "They're waiting."

"For what? They have us surrounded."

Jax was right. They were shrieking, snapping their tentacles like whips in the humid air, bobbing in the river, rising and falling —

— but they were keeping their distance.

"Are they afraid of us?" Marina wondered.

"Maybe. Although I don't know why. Let's walk."

"Where?"

"Back to camp. Right through them."

"Are you crazy?"

"Don't hurt them, don't talk loudly or move quickly, don't look them in the eyes. Be — respectful."

Respectful? Marina almost shouted the word but held it back.

Jax could read her mind. "It's either that or stay right here and let *them* decide what to do. Can you walk?"

"I will," Marina vowed.

"Then let's go."

She took a cautious step forward. Jax leaned away from her. He intertwined his fingers with hers, as if they were simply taking a quiet walk along a river.

One step, two, three …

The creatures oozed around them, their tentacles forming a complex web in the air. Marina's heart raced as they slowly drew toward the monsters.

Their tentacles were in striking distance.

She felt Jax squeeze her hand. She squeezed his in return.

Without a word, they walked into the slimy wall of living beings. The creatures parted for a moment, as if to let them pass, then pressed around them, engulfing them.

Marina felt as if she were drowning — again — in a thick mucous. The eyes she was told to avoid seemed everywhere, a green constellation of eyes searching, watching with sick curiosity.

The creatures pressed inward, fusing with each other, crushing Marina.

So the plan didn't work, she thought bitterly.

At least she had Jax.

She felt his hand tugging away from her. She pulled with all her might. Twenty green eyes rolled around her wrist.

She couldn't have cried out to him, even if she wanted. The ooze pressed against her throat.

She felt Jax's hand slip away.

He was gone.

Chapter 4

Marina managed to slide her hand down to the sheath on her hip. She touched the knife she had taken from Jax and tightened her grip around the handle.

Every thought, every instinct told her to lash out, fight to the death. These creatures were vulnerable — she had stabbed one during her struggle in the river.

Her mind, heart, body and spirit focused on one word:

Fight!

Her brothers had taught her how to defend herself at an early age. Her brother Mer would distract her while Isthen jumped from a hidden corner of the house or stable. He would knock Marina to the ground and playfully choke her. Mer and Isthen laughed and laughed at their game. One day, in the woodlands, they dropped from trees in front of her and behind her. She knew she would lose once again if she let them get close to her. She saw a fallen branch near her. Marina grabbed the branch and with a fury that even startled her, she struck Isthen on the head and Mer in the stomach. She used the branch to vault over their fallen bodies and stood ready to fight.

Isthen and Mer left her alone. "You are a warrior now," Isthen said, gingerly touching the lump swelling on his head.

A warrior.

The only way to survive was to strike quickly.

But Jax —

The oozing creatures lifted her off the ground. Marina

dropped the knife. She cursed Jax, cursed the thought and hesitation. Her chance to lash out was lost.

Floating eyes rolled back and forth like green debris washing ashore in high tide. She felt as if she were in a shipwreck, lost, tumbling, a force beyond her own power tossing her through the air.

Air —

She could still breathe. They hadn't suffocated her.

Yet.

She tried to grab something, anything, but her hands slid on the oily bodies of the creatures. She heard shrieking cries, deafening roars — as if an entire race of people were trapped with her and pleading for help.

The more she struggled, the more the pool of ooze carried her away. At one point, she flipped upside-down. She lost her breath, choking and coughing. The creatures chattered. The eyes rolled away from her.

She coughed again, spitting up water. The pressure from the creatures eased slightly.

Once when she was a little girl, she had disobeyed her parents and had run to the sea on her own. Her mother had said something silly about a rip tide drowning people. Marina had sneaked away during chores and retreated to her favorite place along the shoreline, not far from the jetty. The water looked as calm and steady as her father's open hand and as blue and clear as her mother's eyes. Gentle waves lapped the shore. No white caps. A soft breeze tousled her black hair and stroked her ears.

She swam. The water was pure. Surely it wouldn't harm

her. Her toes touched a sandbar. She kicked off the sandbar and swam farther out to sea.

Something jerked her legs. She looked underwater but saw nothing. She tried swimming back to shore, but the rip tide pulled her under. She panicked, splashed, called for help, but there was no help. She was alone. Marina remembered what her mother had said about rip tides. Against all instinct, she had to relax, stop fighting, move with the flow of the water, swim parallel to the shoreline. Marina did so for what seemed like an endless amount of time, but finally, *finally*, the rip tide released her. She swam back to shore. Her father stood there like a monument. He made sure she was all right, then his strong, steady hand punished her for disobeying her mother.

Mother ... Father ...

Am I dying? Marina now thought. *I keep seeing my family ...*

She slid through the punishing mass of creatures, their tentacles twisting like seaweed in a storm.

She coughed repeatedly. Marina stopped fighting the rip-tide pull of the creatures. She felt her body gaining momentum.

She coughed and wheezed and gasped for air. Her body moved faster. She coughed so hard she thought her body might crack open.

The creatures shot her out.

She flew through air — *air!* — and slammed against a crystalline wall. She fell with a hard crash on the back of her neck. The world seemed to burst into millions of rainbows, then change into stars showering from the night sky.

She was barely conscious, barely aware of the fact that the creatures were done with her.

They were slithering away.

She gazed up at the crystal walls which ascended to a shimmering spot of sunlight — as distant as the dream of HayVen.

Marina tried moving, but all she could do was turn her head —— slightly —— left and right.

At least my neck isn't broken ...

It took her a while to realize that the creatures had swum away in the river and had disappeared into the darkness.

Eventually the world stopped spinning around her. Despite the pain, she was able to sit up on one arm. Her throat burned from raw coughing. She coughed again. A slight, dimpled smile appeared on her face.

She realized what had happened.

The creatures had gagged on me and coughed me up.

It didn't take a knife or quarterstaff to fight them. Just — coughing.

I was — what does Terra call it? — a "disease."

It was bitterly entertaining to think that her life, her Sun Cycles on this planet Dulunae, her knowledge, skills and experience were simply a disease to hideous subterranean creatures with hundreds of rolling eyes.

All her knowledge and experience now told her to rest for a moment on the cold, mossy floor of the cave. Regain strength and balance. Clear her mind.

Instead, she slowly rose to find Jax.

Chapter 5

M arina rubbed the back of her neck. Her vision was blurred. She suddenly realized that the creatures had carried her to an unknown corridor in the maze of caves. The ground was slick with moss. The walls were rough quartz, not the polished crystal she had seen earlier. The air smelled of mould and rotten eggs. The bright light had dimmed.

She wanted to call out Jax's name but waited. She listened to the voice of the cave, the whispers and echoes, the hissing and scraping. She thought she heard a distant, low, rhythmic drumming.

Marina took a few careful steps along the slick path. Her legs still burned from the attack of the creature in the stream. Her neck ached. Her head throbbed.

She walked.

Nothing looked familiar. The creatures could not have carried her far; still, she did not recognize a single piece of the cave floor, walls or ceiling.

Marina took a deep, labored breath and slowly released. "I'm on it," she muttered. She carefully entered a chamber of quartz and stone. The ceiling was low, barely higher than her head. There was just enough light for her to see five passageways in the chamber.

The drumming grew louder. The foul odor filled the cave and made her eyes water.

Marina was tempted simply to pick a passageway and charge into it. That was how she made choices. If she faced a deadly new problem, she would handle it.

She missed having her quarterstaff with her. In her haste to run away from the Outcasts and study the underground river, she had left her favorite weapon at camp. Her father had carved it from an ancient tree that grew in front of her home, the same tree she had climbed as a child. The quarterstaff was smooth, lightweight, easy to handle and use. And powerful. She could run with the quarterstaff, stab it into the ground and leap over a large pit. The staff would bend but never break. The quarterstaff helped her fight, tell time and find directions. She once placed it on the ground next to her and the staff had moved overnight, pointing north like a compass needle. Another time, she stood it upon rocky ground and let it drop; the staff pointed like a farmer's arm to underground water.

When she was a child, her father had told her that wood was alive and much smarter than most people he knew. The tree outside their home had lived through hundreds of Sun Cycles, through storm and drought. Its ancient roots had woven a fantastic tapestry beneath the soil that stabilized the tree and sought fresh water in the deepest pockets of earth.

Marina and her father often sat together gazing at the tree in the soft glow of morning light. Once and only once, her father had said, "*Hi l'tarbe sci,*" in the ancient dialect.

The tree knows.

Marina now sat back in the chamber of quartz and laughed bitterly. *Does the tree know where I am? Can my quarterstaff help me now?*

Light faded. The drumming grew louder. The foul air blinded her.

Marina had to move. She crawled towards a passage — the farthest to her right. The light inside was dim and flickering, as if there were candlelight or a faint fire somewhere close. She hated being in tight places. She felt as if she had crawled into the mouth of a giant Shadow Beast, its jutting jaws poised to snap her in half.

Like a Shadow Beast, the walls gushed a sticky green slime on her.

The rocky walls narrowed like the tip of a cone to a single point of dull green light. Marina crawled backwards, easing her way from the dead end.

She returned to the first chamber and sat — anger and frustration burning across her face to the tips of her ears. She wiped slime from her nose and cheeks.

"Some scout I am."

She slid her fingers up her long ears, the ears she had grown to hate. During the Quae Festival in her community, many young women proudly tied back their hair and adorned their ears with tiny, rainbow-colored seashells as a sign of their beauty. With the Outcasts, she was a freak with ears "the size of big fat hands," as one of the children repeatedly teased.

Jax had said once, "Your ears are beautiful. Proud and perfect, your finest feature." She thought he had been mocking her and had wanted to hit him on the spot. He continued saying that each person had a gift that needed to be found and used properly. She had dismissed this as more Jax-gibberish.

Now, as she sat in the quartz chamber, eye shut, fingers stroking her ears, she allowed herself two thoughts.

Could these accursed ears be worth anything? Was Jax honestly saying they were beautiful?

The thoughts came like soft fragrance, like healing water. For a moment, the thoughts felt right.

I blinded the one person who ever thought I was — beautiful.

The word "beautiful" hung like a dazzling necklace — best draped on someone like Lynai'seth of perfect skin, long hair and small, normal ears.

Still …

Marina felt something strengthen within her, a determination tightening like a fist. She crept forward on hands and knees and squinted into the dark mists of the four remaining passages. She thought she saw a deep red light in the passage to her far left, as if the eyes of a Shadow Beast were staring at her. The monstrous creatures had shown they could be friendly, but Marina still felt distrustful of creatures capable of their unique brutality. She had seen them attack Antibodies with snarling cruelty and deadly intent.

Shadow Beasts were capable of *killing*.

Marina retreated and crawled to the second passageway. This one looked dark and calm, almost inviting after what she had seen so far. The middle passage dipped at a steep angle, then split into three more passages.

I could be down here forever!

The fourth passage was as gray and dim as a fogbound morning at sea. Colorful lights winked in the distance, as if rainbow crystals had shattered and sprinkled the cave walls. Some of the lights were as green as the eyes of the tentacled monsters.

Marina fought the overwhelming urge to pick a passage and dive into it. She had to save Jax, and her indecisiveness was getting her nowhere.

Marina chose the second chamber on her left, the one promising calm darkness and safe passage. She crawled into the mouth of the tunnel. The cool, smooth floor seemed reassuring. This had to be the right way to go.

She curved right, plunging into darkness. She heard drumming from the depths of the caves, as if she were creeping not through rock but through the heart of something quite alive.

Her hands slid across the cool, slick floor of the cave. So far, no obstructions.

With each movement forward, Marina gained more confidence. The drumming was fading.

"I'm on it," she said, her lips curving in a slight smile.

She thought about the caves she had explored as a child in her Quae Community. The limestone caverns were beautiful with wide, gaping chambers and colorful stalactites and stalagmites projecting from the ceilings and grounds. Ample sunlight filtered through holes, so much so that her family could safely wander through the caves, explore or sit around and even share a meal together. There were no beasts or monsters, only the occasional fish slipping through underground streams, tiny lizards scrabbling along rocks or blind, bloated frogs on the ground.

Blind frogs …

Why was it that her thoughts so easily turned back to Jax? Right now he *could* resemble a blind frog — feeling his way through the caves. Of course, she too might resemble a cave lizard as she crawled along the floor …

What would her parents and brothers have thought of Jax? Would they have laughed at his odd round head and bulging eyes? Would they have rejected someone from outside the Quae Community?

No. They were seafarers. Traders. Her mother, father and brothers had seen a stunning variety of people from distant regions of Dulunae. They had welcomed visitors from as far away as Lynai'seth's Shi'vaal Community into their home. The people of the Shi'vaal Community might never accept Jax, but surely her own family would find something worthy in him. Her brothers might tease her until she waved her quarterstaff at them. Then they would show respect.

If only they were still alive …

What would it be like to treat Jax not as fellow scout but as a *partner?* He honored her intelligence, strength and beauty. Each time she found fault in someone — including herself — he found only goodness; in everyone except Dav'yn, who somehow had become his enemy.

What would it be like to — *kiss* him again, without hitting him?

She had to find out. In this new life of hardship, terror and woe, she had found a moment of happiness. She wanted more.

Marina's heart quickened. In the distance lay a disk of milky white light. It looked like a membrane stretched across an opening, like the white eyelid of a cave frog.

White light!

Escape!

The white disk did not cast illumination on the path ahead of her. It seemed to simply float at the end of the tunnel.

Marina moved more quickly.

The drumming had stopped, but there was a warm gust of air, blowing in her face, through the chambers.

Marina kept crawling, faster and faster.

Her fingertips worked their way along the wet floor. Her knees no longer touched — she was up on the tips of her feet, her powerful leg muscles propelling her through darkness. She focused on the white disk, which grew bigger as she approached.

Marina was staring so intently that she didn't notice the shift in wind. Now, the wind wasn't blowing in her face but striking her back.

The wind wasn't mild but growing in strength.

The wind was —

— *pushing her forward.*

Marina's hand struck loose rock that bounced forward. The rocks didn't strike anything.

They fell somewhere.

Marina tried to stop, but the wind batted her forward. She tried getting her grip. Too late.

The wind slapped her. Marina felt herself slipping.

Then — the floor curved downward. The wind shoved her. She couldn't stop, couldn't grab anything.

"NO!"

Marina slipped off the edge of the cave floor.

Into a bottomless pit.

Chapter 6

Somewhere in the underground maze of crystalline walls, rocky corridors, murky streams and pock-marked plates of basalt and granite, Marina had fallen into a gaping pit. Somewhere else in this maze of river and rock, her fellow scout, Jax, lay flat on his back. His limp body did not move.

The oozing, tentacled creatures had torn him from Marina's firm grip, had lifted him off the ground in the rise and roll of their swollen shapes and tossed him like a twig into an oily black pit.

Then the creatures had slithered off into the shadows.

Jax looked like a cast-off, crumpled doll.

A fly landed on his face, crawling across the bright pink landscape of his left cheek, creeping over his nose to the swollen mass around his right eye. The fly crawled up the black, blue, yellow and green rings of the bruise. Jax did not flinch or bat the fly away.

Something, a foul gust of air, slapped the fly from his face. The same gust of air drew back and forth over Jax in waves, like heavy breath.

Miraculously, his right index finger twitched. Then other fingers. Then his wrist.

Jax moaned. "Uhhhhhh ..."

He slowly regained consciousness. For a moment he thought he was back home in his beloved Kerta Community, awakening from a strange illness or clawing nightmare in which Antibodies had attacked his community and killed his family.

Then he remembered that the attack had not been a dream but something all too real.

Even though he was awakening, all he saw was darkness. A grim realization slid over him like a poisonous liquid —

I'm blind.

He gingerly touched his right eye but winced at the touch. He remembered — *Marina.*

There was no wound to his left eye, but it was equally blind.

He hadn't told any of the Outcasts, but his left eye had slowly been going blind for quite some time. He was suffering from malnutrition. In his Kerta Community, his people lived on grains, fresh vegetables and fruits harvested from the rich, spring-fed soils. Long ago, eating animal flesh had been forbidden by their religion. Through time, though, avoiding all meats simply became part of the Kerta culture. Eating animals was looked down upon as barbaric, the stuff of wild tribes.

Jax's people lived on orange vegetables, *kyrota,* which strengthened the body and sharpened the eyesight. He was the only Outcast who could see clearly at night, as if it were as bright as day. The Kertas had two eyelids on each eye. The outer eyelid functioned as protection against bright sun and harsh wind. The inner eyelid was a milky membrane that protected the eye in lower light. At night, Jax could open both eyelids like window blinds and see clearly in darkness. *Kyrota* enhanced this ability.

Now, he lived on stale bread, shrivelled potatoes, roots, berries, insects — whatever the Outcasts could find on their journeys. He hadn't eaten *kyrota* since the Antibody attack on his community, and he was paying the price: blindness in his left eye as sinister as disease.

Jax struggled and propped himself up on an elbow.

"Marina?" he called.

No answer. Only the rhythmic drumming of the earth.

Jax slowly inhaled, coughed and exhaled.

"Marina?"

Nothing.

No sarcastic remarks, no battle cry of "I'm on it!" no quarterstaff whizzing through the air.

I lost her.

His mind turned to the Outcasts, to Lynai'seth and the children. He was supposed to be their scout!

I lost them too ...

"MARINA!"

His voice lifted into the darkness like a bat.

He had survived Antibodies. He had survived Shadow Beasts and the oozing monsters in the caves. He had saved Marina from drowning, had put his lips to hers to revive her and — *there.* He found his crime. He had saved her by using Terra's technique of "resuscitation." The method had worked — Marina, nearly dead, had come back to life. In his delight, Jax had pressed his lips to hers again, not to offer medical help but to — *kiss* her.

The touch had struck like lightning. There had been something shockingly fantastic about kissing Marina. It tasted of wild strawberry and mango. It tingled. It felt like celebration in a world gone mad.

And it was forbidden to kiss before marriage betrothal. Both in his culture and in Marina's.

Worst of all — in that moment with Marina — he had felt no shame, only a leaping joy. Jax had thought that his heart belonged to Lynai'seth, but he now knew that he admired her from a distance the way one admired a masterpiece painting, a sculpture, a soft setting of the twin moons of Dulunae. With Marina, his feelings were as close and warm and real as the touch of her lips.

With his crime came her punishment — a swift fist to his right eye.

I deserved it.

He had tried joking with her to hide his feelings after the kiss and the fist. Had he fooled her? If she suspected his true emotions, there was no telling what she might have done …

Enough.

Jax shifted and sat up. He slowly rose to his feet, feeling a spin of dizziness.

He extended his hands into empty air.

He took a cautious step. Another. Then stumbled and fell to his knees.

"Some scout I am."

He stood again. This time he listened. He heard drumming deep below. He smelled a foul odor like huge heaps of rotten fruit. He felt warm air stroke his face.

He took a single, wobbly step forward, like a baby. Solid ground. Another step. More solid ground.

He decided to take off his wet boots and use his bare feet to guide his way through darkness.

Smooth, cool stone. Then warm rock. Then a hole.

Jax took several confident steps. He tucked his boots under his left arm and swung his right arm back and forth in the air.

A brittle shriek punctuated the low drumming. Another shriek. The multi-faced monsters were still out there. Somewhere.

Jax had no choice but to move forward. They might attack again, they might kill him — but anything was better than lying on his back, worthless.

He stepped downward. His feet touched something fuzzy and soft. Jax squatted and ran his hand along the ground.

Moss.

He was near the underground river. He grabbed some pebbles and tossed them ahead of him. They rattled on rock. He took a stone and threw it. It whizzed through the air, struck a wall, ricocheted and fell to the ground.

He adjusted his angle and threw another rock. It shot through the air, then made the wet sound of a splash.

It IS the river!

Jax's heart leapt at the first sign of hope. He slipped on his boots. He may have been blind, but the river served as a marker as clear as a pointing finger. The river led back to the Outcast camp. He could find Gyro and have him lead a team to save Marina. Gyro had formed the Outcasts, going from community to community on bold rescue missions. He would find Marina in no time. Then Terra, the healer, would restore his sight.

Jax would never profess his shameful feelings of joy, but he would be able to see Marina again, her proud face and thick black hair, her glistening blue-green skin and magical ears. They would be a team again, leading the Outcasts to HayVen. With luck, his nemesis, Dav'yn, would regret joining the Outcasts and would move on to darker facets of his private world of evil.

At that moment, Jax felt anything was possible.

Lost in his thoughts, Jax failed to realize that the shrieking had grown louder. Tearing through the hideous squealing was a deeper snarling. Had he been paying attention, Jax would have recognized the snarling.

Shadow Beasts.

The shrieking and snarling rolled into a single fevered sound, as if the tentacled monsters and Shadow Beasts had attacked each other.

All Jax knew was that a powerful force struck from behind, sending him tumbling forward, down a slope, face-first into the water.

In his blindness, Jax couldn't determine which way was up or down in the water. He panicked and kicked and flapped his arms. The last of his remaining breath rose in bubbles to the surface.

Drowning —

He stopped kicking and arched his back. He felt his body rise. He let his body seek the surface. Jax was able to lift his head. He gasped, spat water, sucked air into his lungs.

Can't swim —

He frog-kicked and slapped the water and managed to get back to the edge of the river where he clung to the rock like a barnacle. He coughed and breathed in and out the thick river air.

He heard fighting along the river, so close that he feared raising his head or lifting an arm too far out of the water.

The river points like a finger …

He couldn't swim, but Jax was able to work his way along the side of the river using his arms and legs. He paused to determine the direction of the river. He knew that the river had been flowing away from the Outcast camp to the point where he had found Marina.

Jax felt a mild current pushing past him. He was headed upstream, towards the camp. He worked his way hand over hand, grabbing rocks, pressing his feet against the river wall. The attack of the Shadow Beasts against the shrieking monsters was louder, more fierce. Even if Jax found the camp, he feared that the Outcasts had run off to another place of safety.

"Gyro!" he cried. "GYRO!"

His voice drew unwanted attention. Something slapped the water next to him. He bit his lip and waited. Then continued moving along the river wall.

It sounded as if a boulder had fallen into the water. There was a thick splash, then pounding and slapping. Creatures were battling in the churning water.

Jax hurried along the river wall, moving upstream. A part of him was grateful that he couldn't see what was happening around him.

Another splash, more thrashing in the water. At first, Jax failed to notice a subtle shift in the texture of sound around him. There wasn't the deep pounding of creatures in a narrow cavern space. There was a crisp escape of noise — up crystalline walls.

He now heard the crystal shattering like frail glass.

He was near the camp.

"GYRO!"

All hope clung to that one word.

"GYRO!"

No answer. He heard the wicked slap of tentacles on the water.

Then a *woosh* and snap, as if a Shadow Beast had tried to bite him.

If there *were* Shadow Beasts and oozing monsters nearby, they were turning their attention towards *him*.

Great! They're ganging up against me!

More creatures dropped like rocks in the water. Something was swimming towards him.

Not just one. Two, three, who knows …

Jax knew his luck was gone, his life was over. Even though no one would see him — no one might ever find him — he decided to fight to the last breath.

He needed to be back on land. He hoisted himself out of the water just as giant jaws snapped near his head. Jax rolled on his side and stood.

Through the noise, the brute howling and repeated shrieking, he heard something that didn't make sense. A lone repetition, a clicking.

He moved toward the sound, perhaps the last sound he would ever hear in his life.

The rapping grew louder. Louder. Jax had no idea what it was. He lunged towards the noise and grabbed something. It was cold and rigid, like — bone.

The unthinkable burst in his mind like volcanic flame: he feared that Shadow Beasts had attacked the Outcasts in the same way that they had attacked the Antibodies. The Outcasts couldn't escape. And the bone he now tugged — wasn't some*thing*. It was some*one*.

"NO!"

He grabbed the bone and wrestled with whatever was pulling it at the other end.

"LET GO!"

He would not let bones be desecrated by wild animals.

"LET GO!"

With a burning strength beyond understanding, Jax wrenched the bone free. The wild shrieking told him he had been in a tug-of-war with a tentacled monster.

Jax swung the bone wildly, striking the pulpy bodies of the monsters. They cried out in pain.

When he heard snarling behind him, Jax spun around and pounded the head of a Shadow Beast. It raged; he struck again and again.

Jax spun around and around, blindly fighting the circle of creatures tightening around him.

His arm muscles felt as if they were becoming paralyzed with pain and final fatigue. He thought a poisonous tentacle had struck him.

The bone whistled as he swung it, as if it had decided to continue the fight on its own. It was impossibly sturdy against the onslaught. More than Jax was. His eyes burned, his chest heaved, his lungs felt on fire. His muscles and will weakened.

The bone swung about, plunging into shrieking ooze, smacking against the head and jaw of a Shadow Beast. The Shadow Beast whimpered, stumbled and slid into the river.

The bone in Jax's aching hand whirred and whistled, but not in defense against monster and beast.

It was on the *attack*.

The bone smashed against another Shadow Beast, which tottered and fell into the river with the first one. Other creatures either fell or dove into the water.

Through the searing pain, Jax sensed something as tiny as hope in this bleak and blooded world.

The focus of the fight was shifting. It was moving away from him and into the river. The oozing monsters wrapped their tentacles around the wounded Shadow Beasts and began sucking the life out of them. Other Shadow Beasts jumped into the water to defend their pack.

Jax took the moment to swing the bone against the rocky floor and crystal wall in a mad attempt to find an escape route. He struck the cave floor, his feet slipping on wet river rock.

He smacked the floor repeatedly, tapping out a path to safety.

The bone seemed to steer him.

Blindly, Jax followed.

Chapter 7

The world underground had run riot.

Coiling green tentacles slammed the water. Shadow Beasts wailed in pain. Their jaws snapped tentacles in half. The river churned and foamed. The air rattled with ear-shattering shrieks.

The fight of Shadow Beasts and tentacled monsters stirred creatures that normally rested quietly in nooks and crannies throughout the caves. Bats with razor claws sliced knife-like along the cave ceilings, darting with uncanny precision and deadly intent. The bats stirred the Nocturnes — birds with black wings, bright green bodies and curling claws. The Nocturnes criss-crossed through the flight of bats, picking at them as they flew.

The commotion alerted giant snakes, each with one un-blinking eye. They oozed from holes in the cave walls, dripping like oily poison into hidden corners of the river, swimming to feast on the carnage.

Rats clicked along the cave floors to bite the one-eyed snakes.

Spidery creatures called Octinids watched from their webs, waiting with profound patience to seize what was left from the battle.

Somewhere in this underworld, a deep, seemingly bottom-less pit breathed like an impossibly vast throat, in and out, in and out. A brilliant red Octinid in an intricate web felt a tug on its webbing as the pit inhaled. The Octinid excitedly hurried to the edge of the web, thinking it had trapped gigantic prey. The pit inhaled, the web snapped, and the creature fell into ultimate darkness.

The Octinid twisted, regained balance and dropped with feather lightness on a tangled black nest. It studied the nest, then crawled to the wall of the deep pit. It climbed and disappeared.

The nest was Marina's thick hair. The Octinid had fallen on her head.

Marina slowly stirred. She sat stunned on a ledge along the wall of the pit. The ledge wasn't much longer than the length of her legs as she sat. The exhaling pit blew foul, warm air on her. Her hair fluttered like the wings of a wounded blackbird.

Marina felt exhausted. Beaten. She had failed to find safe passage through any of the five corridors.

She had failed the Outcasts.

Jax ...

She couldn't bear the thought of him blind and helpless in these deadly caves.

The Outcasts had believed this underground realm would bring shelter and safety. They had found food and water. They were hidden — so they had thought — from threatening beasts.

Marina had allowed herself to be dazzled by the rainbow splendor of the crystal walls and the dappling light of the underground stream. She had selfishly left the Outcast camp, not to find HayVen, but to indulge herself with swimming. The water had been clear and cool, healing her weary body. The fantastic fish had been enticing.

For precious moments in the river, she had pretended to be home in the Quae Community. Marina could imagine her mother calling her to a grand fish and rice dinner. She could hear her father laughing at his own jokes. She could see her brothers playfully fighting to feed the dog scraps of fish under the table.

Food.

Marina's stomach tightened and moaned at the thought of food. When was the last time she'd had anything to eat? Her last meal had been a mouthful of river water during the attack of the tentacled monster.

She looked up over her shoulder at the wall of rock. There were lumps of stone and pockmarks. If she was clever, she could scale the wall to the top of the pit.

"I'm — on it," she said, slowly standing. She felt dizzy. Marina looked down — only once — into the pit.

She placed a foot into a pockmark in the wall, reached out and grabbed the protruding stone. She moved her other leg into position.

Marina began to climb.

The winds from the pit tore at her. She managed to get a foothold. Another.

Higher, higher ...

She slipped.

She regained her balance, then climbed slowly up the sheer face of the wall.

A slap of air knocked her hand loose. She struggled to keep what little balance she had.

Higher ...

The force of the wind increased, as if the pit were determined to knock her from the wall and devour her like an animal.

Her hair fluttered about her. Her arms and legs strained from the exertion. She had to hold on tightly and climb at the same time.

Higher ...

She saw the top of the pit.

Closer ...

As she reached, hundreds of crimson Octinids descended on her, crawling in her hair, on her face. They slid down her back.

They began forming webs on her.

"Get off me!"

Marina batted Octinids from her face. As she reached for the edge of the pit, Octinids swarmed on her hand. The webbing stuck to her skin, forming over her mouth like a choking cloth.

Marina fought against webs and wind. In a final surge of strength, she hoisted herself over the top of the pit. Thousands of Octinids crawled on the ground and cave walls. The chamber quivered in a blood-red mass. Some of the Octinids worked with military precision to form a single web as thick as rope around her neck.

The webbing was strangling her.

Marina worked her fingers under the webbing at her throat. She took a breath and plunged headlong out of the passageway, her feet crunching on red Octinids. Part of the webbing around her neck had yet to harden, and Marina snapped free. She scurried down the passage and returned to the chamber from which she had started. She leaned against the wall to catch her breath.

The Octinids hadn't followed her.

Yet.

Marina shut her eyes. A powerful feeling gnawed at her. *Despair.*

She had never known despair until the Antibodies had attacked her community. They had burned ships, boats and buildings. They had burned the age-old tree in front of her home. They had herded people like sheep into large carts and carried them away to horrid labor camps. They had beaten people and left them for dead. Marina had fought the Antibodies as best she could but almost died, until Gyro appeared and led her to safety.

Now, in the cave, the same fear and despair gripped her heart. There was no exit, no safe passage. Any moment now, the crimson Octinids would catch up with her. If not them, then the tentacled monsters would strike. Or Shadow Beasts.

Her final thoughts were of her family: her mother and father, Fontana and Azur. Brothers Mer and Isthen. Not long ago, in an open plain by the Seven Statues, an Antibody had said that they were still alive. Had this been a lie to further torture her?

Even if it were true, it was too late. She had lost them forever.

Marina thought about Gyro, Terra, S'yen, Klanga and the other Outcasts. Were they safe? Alive? She had to think so. Gyro was highly resourceful in the most extreme situations. He had saved all of them from certain death at the hand of the Antibodies. He was determined to lead them to HayVen. Gyro had never failed, and he wasn't about to now.

Marina looked. The first of the red Octinids appeared at her feet.

She thought about Jax. She had not liked him at first. He had that round pink head like a ripe melon and huge fish eyes that seemed to stare right through her. He talked too much. He always seemed nervous and unsure. He kept asking her questions about herself and about her family. He listened to everything she said. He had opinions.

He said I was beautiful.

Even though she shouldn't have, she thought about the kiss. It was a moment of bliss that changed their lives.

It was a moment gone.

He has to be alive.

He has to ...

Her ear twitched. The caves were wild with noise, but she heard something in the chaos that caught her attention.

Tapping. Three swift beats, three long beats, three short beats.

It might simply have been water dripping on smooth stone. Still, it was the only benign sound she heard.

More Octinids appeared like licks of flame along the ground.

Marina breathed deeply and entered the middle chamber. The ground dropped sharply, leading to three more passage-ways.

The tapping got louder. This could be a good sign, but she doubted it. Most likely the tapping was part of a trap.

She listened carefully. The sound might be the snapping of a Shadow Beast's jaws.

Marina peered down into each of the three passages. The left passage was a deep green fog. The middle chamber was soft brown, dimly lit. Something glittered in the far right passage, shards of light. She used the ears Jax thought beautiful and listened intently for any clue.

Tap, tap, tap ...

Marina sat back, studied the three passages and listened with all of her might. Beads of sweat appeared on her forehead as she concentrated.

Minutes passed.

Crimson Octinids appeared.

Marina made her choice. She dove into the unknown.

Chapter 8

"Marina is DEAD!"

"Jax is DEAD!"

"They are not!"

"They are too!"

"Where's Marina? I want Marina!"

"She has funny ears!"

"Well, Jax has funny eyes!"

Dav'yn sat on a jagged rock scratching the bandages on his hands. "Stop talking!" he snapped at the Outcast children. For some reason, they followed him like gnats.

The day had fallen into fitful evening. The clouds in the western sky crumbled into copper dust. The twin moons of Dulunae peeked in the east.

Little Klanga held her pet, Feelie, close to her round face. Feelie tightened into a bright, orange ball of fur, tucking his paws into his body. "But Jax isn't coming back," she said, stroking Feelie's fur.

"No loss," Dav'yn muttered under his breath.

"Or Marina."

"Now *there* is a loss," he said. "Her death will release me from her debt, though."

"What?"

"Nothing. Now be quiet or monsters will tear all of you limb from limb."

The children shrieked. The twins, Alamine and Amina, began crying.

"The monsters love crying," Dav'yn said. "They listen for children who cry, then eat them in their sleep."

"Oh!" The twins sniffled, coughed and finally grew still. They hurried with the others to another part of the camp where Lynai'seth sat. She extended her arms in greeting.

The Outcasts had fled from the caves and now sat on a rocky plateau overlooking the surrounding hillside and plains. Gyro had wanted to stay underground and wait for Marina and Jax, but Dav'yn had convinced Gyro to lead the Outcasts to higher ground.

Gyro argued with him but finally agreed.

Before they had fled from the caves, Dav'yn had tried taking Marina's quarterstaff, which lay propped on a small rock. The staff was a formidable weapon. He grabbed it, but the quarterstaff burned his hands. Dav'yn recoiled in pain, his curses echoing in the caves. "*Mephiste!*" he shouted again and again.

The healer Terra had managed to rub an aloe ointment on the burns and wrapped his hands with bandages. Dav'yn cursed under his breath —

— And left the quarterstaff in the caves.

Now, as he sat on the plateau, Dav'yn looked down on the cave entrance in the distance. Terra joined him. She had a bright blue gemstone embedded in her forehead, deeply-set slanted eyes and six fingers on each hand. He knew nothing of her tribe and bore no resemblance to her. He had tough red skin and patches of black hair. He had an oversized skull — which, he said, contained his oversized brain — long, wiry arms and thin legs.

"How's the patient?" Terra asked, taking his right hand without permission.

"Burning with anger."

"Marina's quarterstaff really did this to you?"

"It must have been sitting on hot volcanic rock."

"Of course. And wood conducts volcanic heat," she said.

"It can."

Terra smiled. "Your science is interesting."

"This, from someone who uses fairy tale concoctions."

Dav'yn looked over Terra's shoulder at her open bag of supplies. He saw glass bottles filled with blue liquids, brown salves, orange ointments and pink powders that she had ground with a mortar and pestle.

Terra carefully peeled the bandages from his hands and reapplied aloe ointment. "My fairy tale medicines are keeping the skin from falling off your hands."

"It must be my own healing abilities. I grew up in the desert."

"So I've heard, at least fifty or sixty times."

"You learn slowly."

Dav'yn watched as her fingers crawled over his forearms like a desert spider. He had to admit she was somewhat skilled, but she laughed and smiled too much to his liking. He was comforted by the fact that good humor was the simplest luxury to steal and destroy. These were vicious times. Only the hard-hearted survived.

A tall gangly boy named Oolo appeared. Dav'yn snorted. Oolo served no purpose.

"Something important I must say, something that will change your day. It —" Oolo paused. His gaze focused on a multi-legged insect the size of a human finger. Oolo picked it up. The creature wriggled helplessly. He opened his mouth and bit the insect. A green juice spurted on his chin. Oolo chewed and swallowed.

"So ideal, a tasty meal," he said, wiping his sleeve across his mouth.

"Oolo," Terra said, "what is your message?"

"You speak but don't say. Please don't play."

"You had a message you wanted to share — tell us now, if you dare."

Oolo smiled. "Now you make sense. Gyro is waiting, let us go hence."

He spun, stumbled, bounced off a rock and disappeared.

Dav'yn grunted. "He's such a waste."

Terra finished with his wrappings. "You speak in haste."

"Stop talking that way!"

"Don't you want to play?"

"*Mephiste ska te,*" Dav'yn said.

"That didn't sound okay."

Dav'yn grinned crookedly, his sharp canine teeth appearing in white spikes.

They joined the others who had gathered around a small fire. A boy named Ignis had used two of his Fire Sticks, thin strips of wood that burned with a small, intense flame. The Outcasts had warmth and adequate light without revealing their position to enemies.

Gyro was the last to sit among the group.

Lynai'seth had the task of quieting the thirteen children.

Two places were left empty for Marina and Jax.

A young man named Yan documented the travels of the Outcasts. He opened a large, leather book on his lap and began to write. Yan was from a reclusive mountain community given to deep meditations and fantastic dreams. Dav'yn distrusted Yan. Gyro had relied on Yan's visions to find HayVen — and here they sat, on cold rock in the middle of nowhere, food in short supply, two scouts left for dead.

Gyro waited for the children to settle. Lynai'seth seemed to be having a difficult time calming them. Dav'yn hated the noise — each extra sound revealed their location to predators.

Alamine and Amina began crying again. Klanga squeezed Feelie. Ru'an made a chirping noise. A small boy, named Kg, twitched. He suffered from a crippling disease that affected his brain and muscles.

"Enough!" Dav'yn cried.

Lynai'seth walked in a circle around the children. Her head was bowed. She looked tired. Lynai'seth took a deep breath. There was a catch in her throat. She released a single, pure, melodic note. The song grew more complicated, more ornate, like a single caterpillar suddenly taking flight as a handful of bright butterflies.

The children cried.

Dav'yn shifted fitfully. "Why can't she make them stop?"

"Because you're shouting at them," Terra said. "Be quiet or my medicines will turn your skin bright pink like Jax."

"NO!"

"I think it would suit you."

"ENOUGH!"

Lynai'seth paused, breathed deeply, and sang again. The melody was delicate, soft as two shadows folding into night.

The children calmed.

Gyro stared at the ground. He ran his finger in the dust as if devising a plan. He was the oldest member of the Outcasts, the first one to survive Antibody attacks and rescue the others. He had dark, almond-shaped eyes, a strong face and thin beard. Although he was heavy set and muscular, he moved with quick, easy confidence.

His skin color changed with his moods. Most of the time, his deep brown skin tones reflected his cheerful nature. Tonight, his skin tones were muddy green as if a slow poison were overtaking him. His voice, usually loud and brimming with laughter, was low.

"We've lost our scouts," he said.

Dav'yn sat forward. "We know that! And yet we're all still alive."

Gyro ignored him. "We hope they are alive but have to accept the worst. Let us pause and offer a moment of silence in their honor. If you pray to a god, do so; if not, just think about our missing friends."

Some of the children sniffled. Lynai'seth raised a calming hand, but they ignored her.

"She's losing her grip on them," Terra said.

After a pause, Gyro again drew images in the dust. "Friends, we have walked the open plains to the crystal caves. Yan's visions indicated that 'rainbow chambers' might offer passage to our destination. Either the caves were not the 'rainbow chambers' in question, or we have need of redirection."

Dav'yn jumped to his feet. "The scouts lied to us! They misled us! We sat open and vulnerable in the caves! It was fortunate I heard the advance of *monstri umbrae* — Shadow Beasts — in the caves or we would all be dead!"

"The Shadow Beasts helped us fight Antibodies," Terra said. "They saved us. They saved *you,* according to Jax."

Dav'yn ignored her. "Didn't you hear them fighting in the river? Didn't you feel the tremors or see the crystal fall? Some things are *not* to be trusted."

"I won't argue with you there," Terra said.

"Be they *monstri umbrae* or other creatures, we were in danger! Do you deny this? Do you, Leader?"

Gyro shook his head. "No."

"We have the advantage up here. We can see enemies before they attack. We can survey passages to safety. Am I correct?"

"Yes, you are," Gyro said. He turned to Yan. "Do you have any insight as to where we go next?"

Yan had been staring into the small fire. His eyelids fluttered. "*Kleistor,*" he said.

"Use the Common Tongue."

"*Kleistor,*" he repeated, then said no more.

Gyro looked at the Outcasts. The children were sniffling and sobbing. Alamine and Amina held hands. Oolo was digging for insects. Some of the others sat with arms locked around their knees.

"Your Common Tongue is sorely limited," Dav'yn concluded.

Many Sun Cycles ago, a band of elders called the Knowers had travelled from one community to another in an effort to learn about and record the many known cultures and dialects. During that time they created the Common Tongue, a combination of several languages that helped people from different communities speak with each other. The Knowers served as noble educators, patiently "teaching the Tongue," as they had expressed it.

The Common Tongue was easy to learn and use. There were eleven Major Consonants and eleven Major Vowels. Simple dots and curves added to a Major Vowel could change it to a Minor Vowel. The Common Tongue was easy to read and simple to pronounce.

At first, only the younger people spoke the Common Tongue — partly to rebel against their parents, mostly to meet young women and men from other communities.

In bringing the Common Tongue to the various communities, the Knowers had opened new trade routes and had fostered prosperity among the rising merchant classes. They had also brought about the beginning of the end. Many cultures suffered an erosion of their heritage. Children no longer cared about their ancestors' lives or languages.

Gyro promoted the use of the Common Tongue among the Outcasts. Most of the time, this tactic succeeded. Now, under the twin moons, at twilight on the high plains, both Common Tongue and all other languages failed to translate Yan's one cryptic word:

Kleistor.

"It means *nothing*," Dav'yn said sarcastically.

"Yan," Gyro insisted, "explain the word."

Yan shut his eyes.

"I thought he said *H'glestyr,*" Terra commented, "meaning in my language the opposite direction of the Frozen Lands."

Lynai'seth spoke. "In the Shi'vaal Community, *Shi'vastl* means the small rainbows held in morning dew on flowers."

"Rainbows," Gyro said with a faint smile.

"In my community," Dav'yn said, "we ride hump-backed animals called *tshaamo,* and *fecustund* is their dung. Which is all the dreamy boy has offered."

Some of the children giggled.

"That's enough," Gyro said.

Dav'yn circled to stand over him. "We are truly getting nowhere."

Gyro looked up at him. "You're welcome to leave any time you want."

"You'd like that, wouldn't you? I thought you were the Collector of the Lost. You violate your own principles if you cast me out! What then?"

"Why bother with us if we're so wrong all the time? Go off on your own!"

"I was exiled here. I know these lands. You yourselves found me alone in the one safe place by the Seven Statues. Like you, I seek a kingdom. I can lead — help you lead this group to safety."

In darkness, by firelight, Dav'yn's rough words bore a force. He could feel his words taking root like seeds in soil.

While the Outcasts debated, Dav'yn scratched his chin thoughtfully. The art of persuasion required knowing exactly when to be silent.

What he chose not to discuss was what the dreamy boy

Yan and the princess Lynai'seth had accidentally discovered on the Seven Statues.

The word CH'NOPS.

The word itself seemed to mean nothing. It held sway over the Antibodies, effectively paralyzing them during battle.

Thus, CH'NOPS meant power.

Dav'yn cursed himself for not deciphering the word on his own. He had spent enough time among the Seven Statues to discover its existence. The dreamer and the princess had compiled rubbings of the letters from the base of each statue and had composed the word CH'NOPS.

And the word changed everything.

Now that he knew the word, Dav'yn had considered sneaking away in the night. Antibodies would not harm him. Still, *monstri umbrae* had risen from dark mystery to attack them. They had been a valuable ally in a recent escape from Antibodies, but their bloodthirsty howling at night chilled his bones.

So he stayed with the Outcasts. They had proven themselves useful, offering safety in numbers. He had never seen a warrior as skilled as his Master, Marina. Her loss had been a setback for him.

The loss of the Pink Boy, the one they called Jax, filled him with hope. One less enemy in the world was a good thing indeed.

Debate continued around the campfire. Gyro eyed Dav'yn. The fact that the Outcasts were debating at all was a victory for Dav'yn. They were taking his words seriously.

I have plans for all of you, Dav'yn thought, a gleam in his eye.

Ignis lit another Fire Stick. Lynai'seth excused herself and took the children to their covered carts where they slept under thin blankets.

Yan wrote furiously in his book. Dav'yn peeked over his shoulder.

Much of the writing was in the Common Tongue.

Dav'yn read. He suddenly realized that the book was dangerous.

Yan's book compiled their history, and history offered perspective and wisdom. History recorded past mistakes, providing gifts to people smart enough to pay attention and not make the same mistakes.

The book contained the science of edible and poisonous plants and insects, the geography of lands Outcasts had already explored, the expressive art of the children, the listing of tribes and languages, maps of the stars and phases of the twin moons. The subjects ranged through space and time.

Dav'yn had learned that, long ago, the Knowers had compiled the same kinds of books and had been killed for their efforts. A fierce desert tribe feared that the Knower books stole their souls. For this, the Knowers had to face the ultimate punishment for their crimes.

Dav'yn's chest tightened as he watched Yan turn a page. The next chapter began with the word CH'NOPS. There were drawings, symbols, charts and mysterious words that could serve as clues.

This book was now priceless to Dav'yn and, for a time at least, the dreamy boy Yan had some value to him. He needed to learn Yan's language.

His attention returned to the debate. "We will keep camp here," Gyro decided. "We will give Marina and Jax one night to find us. No one — I repeat, absolutely no one — goes down into the caves looking for them."

"Your wisdom cannot be measured," Dav'yn said, "but where do we go tomorrow?"

"Southwest."

"And not southeast? Why?"

"That was the direction Yan predicted."

"A pity he's incapable of agreeing with his own predictions now."

They all looked at Yan, who was turning his book sideways to draw something, as a child might.

"Southwest," Gyro said. He stood. Dav'yn had forgotten how tall and powerful Gyro could appear.

"As you wish," Dav'yn said.

Dav'yn returned to the point on the plateau where he could look down at the cave entrance. Lynai'seth was already standing there. Her skin was deep violet, like the evening sky, her long hair luminous as spun gold. She was tightening the braids of her hair. Dav'yn noticed that the hair bands she used bore the same symbols as the cuffs and hem of her long dress. Despite their many trials and travels, her dress was never soiled.

"Any signs?" he asked.

Lynai'seth did not answer. As she worked on a braid, her sleeve dropped from her wrist, revealing an intricate tattoo that also resembled the symbols of her garment.

She looked like a living language.

"A pity we lost the Master. She was a skilled fighter."

Lynai'seth turned on him. He was startled. The pupils in her eyes had vanished. Her eyes were completely white, as white as the twin moons. "They're still alive."

Dav'yn grinned. "I hadn't guessed you to be a romantic. I've seen you reject the Round-Headed Boy."

If it was possible, Lynai'seth's eyes grew even whiter with anger.

"You seem wise and practical," Dav'yn said. "Like me."

"I am nothing like you."

"I've already had more words with you than the Round-Headed Boy ever did."

Lynai'seth's eyes burned with the intensity of white flame. Then something seemed to burst, as if in a strike of lightning.

When his vision cleared, Dav'yn found himself flat on his back, bones aching. Lynai'seth towered over him. He tried to speak but could only babble.

Even the best warriors know when to retreat, he thought, crawling away from her.

He crept across the plateau, finally hiding in his corner by the supply cart. He pulled his blanket up over him but peeked over the edge to see if Lynai'seth had followed him.

Lynai'seth stood in the distance, in moonlight, as still as stone.

Chapter 9

As Dav'yn drifted to sleep, Lynai'seth studied the night. A soft breeze wafted past her, stroking her hair and face. Shooting stars slashed the black sky.

In the distance, there was howling. Mournful, as if a wounded creature were crying out from a loss of life.

Quiet.

A tumble of rock.

Lynai'seth turned.

Two red eyes appeared down by the cave entrance. A Shadow Beast. The eyes stared, then melted into the night. They reappeared in another pocket of shadows, then another, as if the creature were circling their camp.

Then, darkness.

Lynai'seth spent the night watching for signs of life.

Wisps of steam rose from the ground, licked the cool night air and vanished.

The eyes of Shadow Beasts seemed everywhere, blinking in a blood-red constellation along the rim of rocks, along the ground, across the rutted earth. The Shadow Beasts howled with brutal abandon.

Lynai'seth shivered. She pinched the collar of her garment around her neck.

The twin moons of Dulunae drifted like eyes across the night sky, ever watchful of the world below.

Klanga whined from a bad dream. She shifted fitfully in her cart, then settled.

Yan drifted past Lynai'seth. He did not look at her or speak. He carried his book under his arm, wandered, then huddled in a corner by a spike of rock.

Milky moonlight washed the cave entrance. There were hundreds of footprints, as if an army had secretly shuffled through the night landscape to hide in the crystal caves.

All at once, the rising steam, the eyes of the Shadow Beasts — all signs of chaos and commotion disappeared.

Silence hovered like a breath held in fear. This was not the silence of peace but a pause before catastrophe.

Silence …

Then the world within the maze of caves seemed to erupt.

The earth trembled and cracked open. In a roar and rumble of rock, boulders tore from their ancient stations on the hillside, rolled downward, and crashed. The rock showered on the cave entrance and continued falling in a grim avalanche — tumbling, smashing, shattering to bits.

The Outcasts were on their feet, watching with Lynai'seth from the safety of their plateau. The children ran to her, screaming.

"We're going to die!" a child cried.

Gyro gasped. "No!"

The children clutched each other and watched in horror as the avalanche continued its furious attack on the cave entrance, impossibly large boulders bouncing like pebbles to the ground.

The avalanche ended as quickly as it had begun. Dust swirled, chips of rock clattered and came to rest. When the dust cleared, a new nightmare revealed itself.

Even if Marina and Jax had somehow survived their ordeals, they would not be able to escape from the caves.

The rock rested against the cave entrance with the finality of a tombstone.

Chapter 10

The eye of the morning sun was dim and distant. A deep mist clung to the surrounding landscape. The cave entrance was lost.

There was rumbling in the sky, as if a storm were approaching.

Before breaking camp, the Outcasts continued to argue about direction. Dav'yn insisted they head southeast. Some of the Outcasts wanted to return to the shrine of the Seven Statues, where they had been surrounded by the dreaded Antibodies but had survived. Still others wanted to stay exactly where they were, on high ground.

Gyro repeatedly asked Yan for guidance, but Yan remained silent, his eyes shut in a trance. Gyro remained fixed on his decision to head southwest.

"We'll leave now and use the fog as cover," he said. "We can't risk waiting for any more tremors."

"We *must* wait," Dav'yn countered. "We could easily get lost down there."

"I know the way."

"Do you?"

"Dav'yn, you're welcome to choose your own route at your own time."

"Leader, I choose the path of wisdom," he said.

Lynai'seth, usually patient, snapped at the children. They whined, they cried. The boy Kg sat on the ground, rocking back and forth. Lynai'seth lifted him, and he struggled in her arms. She carried him to a cart and forcefully placed him in it. Kg moaned.

Terra joined Lynai'seth. "I'm sorry," she said.

"The children will be fine. They're tired and hungry."

"You spoke to me! In Common Tongue!"

Lynai'seth had broken the long silence she had been keeping since joining the Outcasts. Her voice, though tired, carried a musical lightness to it. "These are drastic times."

"I'm sorry about Marina and Jax."

Lynai'seth shut her eyes and bowed her head.

"The thing is," Terra said, "I don't feel that they're dead."

Lynai'seth looked at her.

"In my community of healers," Terra explained, "the most skilled could actually *feel* the pain of a patient. If a patient had broken his leg, the healer would also feel it in her leg. In this way, her medicine was accurate, powerful — and quick." Terra smiled slightly.

"That sounds more like a curse than a blessing," Lynai'seth said. "Can *you* feel other people's pain?"

"Sometimes, when I shut my eyes and concentrate. Last night, I focused on Marina. My throat grew tight, as if something had been choking her."

"Did you think about Jax?"

"Yes." Terra paused.

"And …"

"The pain was so sharp that I jumped up. I looked at the sky, but I couldn't see anything."

"It was night time."

"No — I couldn't see a thing. Not even the moons."

"Like … death," Lynai'seth said. She paused. "Do you really think he's still alive?"

"I think he's more resourceful than we all give him credit for," Terra said. "He doesn't act as quickly as Marina, but he studies everything. He thinks deeply. He feels deeply."

"I've never met anyone like him."

"Marina, on the other hand, acts when she needs to — with force and fury. They make a good team — brains and brawn."

Lynai'seth closed her eyes and whispered something, perhaps a prayer. She changed the subject. "Which direction do you think we should take?"

"I think we should all keep together. If Gyro says southwest, we go southwest."

"You believe that's the right way to go?"

"I believe it's the way of hope. My community sought two paths in life: to pain or to promise. Gyro offers promise."

"But haven't you noticed anything about him?"

"Yes, he —"

S'yen of the Avian Community interrupted her. "*Kscree d'yoh kehtch! Kscree d'yoh kehtch!*" he cried. S'yen had thick tangled hair, an angular face and a beak-like nose. He wore a lightweight chain mail vest, adorned with large brown-and-white feathers. As she spoke, he flapped his arms like a bird.

The young girl he had rescued from his community, Ru'an, was by his side. She was equally agitated. "*Kscree!*"

"What is it?" Lynai'seth said.

"*Kscree!*" S'yen and Ru'an both shouted.

"I don't understand you," Terra said. "What are you trying

to say? Use the Common Tongue!"

S'yen tucked his hands under his arms and bobbed his head.

"*Kscree!*"

Lynai'seth knelt before Ru'an. "Use the words I taught you." Ru'an's young body shivered. She rattled on in Avian language.

Lynai'seth looked up. "Can't anyone translate what they're saying?"

"Jax could," Terra said.

"Where's Xalid? Doesn't he speak five languages?"

"Not Avian."

"Ask him!"

Terra hurried through the camp. Everyone was getting ready for the next part of the journey. There was no excitement, no laughter, only a dim, dutiful silence.

She found Xalid under a supply cart. He was studying the axles. Xalid had black hair, a proud face and long arms. He was skinny, too skinny from hunger. His skin looked as gray as ash.

Xalid was from the Community of D'arbz'zya. He had said he was a descendant of the Knowers, most of whom had been exterminated long ago, but had managed to raise several heirs in secret.

Terra spoke to him in his native tongue.

"*Shisti'be'i'dem,*" she said, meaning, "May you know goodness in your day."

"*Xan'tias'ti,*" he said, thanking her.

She asked if he spoke Avian. "*Xdisti'E'Avia'qa'lhoqor?*"

"*B'ntyet.*" Not enough to make sense.

Terra said that S'yen was troubled about something. Xalid replied that he wanted to help but had to check the carts. Time was of the essence.

Gyro was calling for the Outcasts to take formation. He had divided the rest of them into groups of four. Each group was responsible for a cart: food, water, tools, weapons, shelter, clothing and general supplies. The Outcasts used their own braided rope made from vines or plant fibers to secure canvas over the carts.

Lynai'seth was in charge of the two carts that the children used. Outcasts, such as Xalid, checked the wheels, axles, side panels, beds, seats, coverings and steering handles for damage. If required, the Outcasts could break camp quickly and move into formation without much direction, but they badly needed four-legged animals, such as horses, to pull the carts. They had not been able to capture any during their quest.

Terra pulled a long needle from her kit and rubbed it repeatedly in one direction with a small piece of silk. She tied a piece of thread to the middle of the needle and held it up at eye level.

The needle, now magnetized, pointed north. Terra smiled, and Gyro nodded to her.

They slowly headed southwest from the plateau.

Gyro led, taking up the handles of the first cart. Dav'yn walked a pace behind him and to the left, then wandered back towards Yan to talk about his book.

S'yen and Ru'an continued to call out excitedly in their mysterious language. Terra tried quieting them, with no luck.

Normally, Lynai'seth walked behind the second and third

carts with the children. This time she was last to leave. She adjusted her four hair bands and long, thick braids. She looked off in the direction of the cave entrance, which was obscured by fog. She took a deep breath and released a long, sorrowful note that seemed to lace through the fog and stroke the fallen rock below.

No sign of life.

Of Marina.

Of Jax.

Chapter 11

In the fog, the caravan of Outcasts looked like a great gray snake. The only sounds were the creaking of wooden wheels on the carts. The children slept.

At times it seemed as if Gyro could walk endlessly without rest. He always pulled a cart on his own, as if the very exertion somehow refreshed and strengthened him. In brighter times, he whistled or told long, complicated, humorous stories to entertain the children. Today, he was silent.

"I see deep cracks in the ground," Dav'yn said, circling in front of Gyro, "I hear monsters." He persisted in trying to convince the band of Outcasts to head southeast to safety.

"Why don't you go ahead and scout for us?" Terra asked.

Dav'yn sneered at her. "You'd like that."

"I'd like for you to be quiet."

"I AM quiet!"

"You could awaken the dead. Like Jax."

Dav'yn grew still.

Terra returned to S'yen and Ru'an, who were struggling to keep quiet. Their eyes darted left and right. S'yen repeatedly pointed backwards. In the dense, oppressive fog, Terra saw nothing.

There was an occasional rumbling behind them, as if an aftershock of the earth tremor had struck.

Then, the damp, clinging silence of the mist.

The Outcasts trudged across unknown terrain.

At one point, Gyro whistled two sharp notes. Each cart

leader, in turn, whistled two notes in response. In this way, they signalled that all was well along the caravan.

They walked downhill, along a narrow path between two towering walls of deep black rock. The rocks had been stripped of all vegetation. The wagons bobbled on the uneven passage.

The children stirred, but remained quiet. Their job, more often than not, was to be calm.

"I hear something," Dav'yn said. He turned to Terra. "Don't you?"

"Yes —"

"I knew it!"

"I hear *you.*"

"I'm disturbed."

"I'll say. Why don't you help pull a cart?"

Dav'yn grunted. "That's work for drones. I'm a master of strategy."

"Is that what got you exiled to the desert?"

Dav'yn's eyes widened. "Wizard! Who told you that?"

"You did, at the Council last night."

"I'm too honest for my own good. That has always been my problem."

"We've all been wondering how you wound up in the Shrine of the Seven Antibody Statues by yourself."

"I — awoke there."

"You what?"

"I was part of an escape team when the Antibodies attacked our community. I offered my insight. They hit me on the head and exiled me."

"That's ridiculous."

"I agree. They should have hailed me as leader instead of leaving me in the dust."

"G'unk-g'unk," S'yen called from somewhere in the fog. "*Kscree d'yoh kehtch!*"

"G'unk-g'unk," Terra repeated. "I've heard that somewhere before."

"The Bird Boy is squawking," Dav'yn said. "He needs his seed."

"Bird …" Terra said. "Yes. A type of bird. A —"

Before she could finish, a flock of giant birds thundered behind them. They were not flying but running along the ground. The G'unk-g'unks, as S'yen called them, were as tall as trees, with powerful orange legs, fat, feathered bodies, craning necks, sharp yellow beaks and eyes as hard and gleaming as black diamond. They lurched as they ran, their heads bobbing back and forth, back and forth.

S'yen reached into a cart and slid on his Battle Gloves, each of which had three large claws of curving, unbreakable bone. Ru'an also put on a small pair of gloves and began looping a long strand of rope. She jumped down from the cart and ran ahead of the caravan with S'yen.

"*Kscree! Kscree!*" they both cried.

Gyro hurried to them. "S'yen! You know what these things are?"

"G'unk-g'unk!"

"Common Tongue!"

"Big bird!" Ru'an cried.

"I can see that! What do we do?"

"*Kscree!*" S'yen said.

"What?"

Ru'an drew a breath and shouted. "GATHER BUT DO NOT HARM!"

Gyro watched as S'yen ran off and swung his arms in the air. He was herding some of the G'unk-g'unks. Ru'an tied a loop at the end of her rope, spun it over her head and whipped the rope at the huge bird. It dodged, and the rope fell to the ground. Ru'an quickly gathered the rope and tried again.

Something the Outcasts hadn't seen in a long time — a smile — spread across Gyro's face. He stuck the tips of his thumb and forefinger in his mouth and blew a loud whistle. The leaders of each cart ran to him.

The G'unk-g'unks ran in circles around the caravan. Some of them pecked at the food carts. They flapped their enormous green feathers, stirring clouds of dust.

Dav'yn had drawn his knife. "Kill them!"

"No!" Gyro said.

"They're food!"

"I said NO!" He pointed to S'yen and Ru'an. "Look! They know these animals! S'yen said to gather but do not harm! Respect that! Tu'ghee T'an, get six others. Pull stakes, ropes and wood reflectors from the carts and build a circular fence!"

Tu'ghee T'an and his sister, Lhista T'an, smiled, nodded and set about their task. They were slim and nimble. They never wasted a single movement of their bodies. Their smooth skin looked like a fantastic, peach-colored liquid. Lhista T'an ran for the other Outcasts as Tu'ghee T'an dug into supply carts for fence materials.

Gyro pointed to a boy named Mohir'a'qest. "Get all the

rope you can find! If you can't find much, make some! Now! Get Zwyna to help you!"

Mohir'a'qest grinned. He and a girl named Zwyna often challenged each other to contests. Now they would see who could make rope the fastest.

The G'unk-g'unks stomped in mad circles, pecked at food carts, shoved each other, slapped Outcasts away with their powerful wings.

"Lynai'seth!" Gyro called. "Make sure the children stay in their carts!"

Lynai'seth watched Ru'an and S'yen. "I believe the children can help."

"You're sure about that?"

"Give us a chance."

Gyro looked at Lynai'seth and smiled. "Go!"

Lynai'seth hurried to the carts. She shouted instructions to the children. At first, they trembled, afraid of the giant birds surrounding them. Klanga held Feelie and ran into Lynai'seth's waiting arms. One by one, the children followed. Alamine and Amina promised to keep Feelie close to them. Ingwa, Dalyne and others stood in line as Lynai'seth directed them.

"You lead the children to their deaths!" Dav'yn cried, still wielding his knife.

"Watch and learn," Lynai'seth said.

She led the Outcast children towards the front of the caravan, then out into the open field. Ru'an saw her friends. She smiled and waved to them.

"*Kscree d'yoh kehtch!*" she called to them, which meant, "The birds can help. Gather but do not harm." Even the children who did not speak the Avian language knew exactly what their friend was saying.

On Lynai'seth's orders, they formed a wide circle around S'yen and Ru'an. They imitated S'yen, flapping their arms, calling out to the G'unk-g'unks, chasing the birds.

S'yen looked at Lynai'seth, smiled and nodded his thanks.

Lynai'seth's eyes turned white — not out of anger but inspiration. She tugged and folded her dress into pants legs. She took the rope from Ru'an, stepped forward and watched for a specific G'unk-g'unk — the biggest one, the leader, with a rainbow of rings around its neck.

While the children chased the birds, Lynai'seth spun the rope over her head and whipped it through the air. The rope flew over the G'unk-g'unk's head and slid down its neck. Lynai'seth tightened the rope, pulling on it with all her might. The bird struggled, but Lynai'seth held her ground. Other children lined up behind her and held onto the rope.

The G'unk-g'unk bucked, flapping its huge wings, crying out, its strong legs kicking. It tried jabbing Lynai'seth with its beak, but she dodged it. In one deft move, she flipped up onto the back of the G'unk-g'unk, gathered the rope into her hands and rode the wild animal.

"Wheee!" Klanga cried.

The children cheered.

S'yen was awestruck. Ru'an clapped her hands.

Lynai'seth clamped her legs onto the beast, tightened the rope and struggled to keep her balance. The G'unk-g'unk slammed her into a rock wall, but Lynai'seth held on to the rope.

The other G'unk-g'unks seemed unsure what to do. S'yen used the confusion to herd them towards the fence that Tu'ghee T'an, Lhista T'an and five other Outcasts were hastily pounding into the ground. Zwyna ran and handed out rope. Mohir'a'qest was right behind her, braiding rope while he ran.

Gyro made sure that Terra and other Outcasts were defending the food carts. Three G'unk-g'unks worked in unison to stick their heads under a supply cart and flip it upside-down. Pots, pans, cups, bowls and utensils rattled onto the ground. The G'unk-g'unks stepped on them, crushing some of the clay cups and bowls.

Lynai'seth was riding the G'unk-g'unk leader, but other birds took charge and mounted a counterattack. In groups of three, they lined up side-by-side, charged the carts and knocked them over. Gyro and other Outcasts ran back and forth, swinging sticks at the G'unk-g'unks.

"Terra!" Gyro called as a G'unk-g'unk clamped its beak around his forearm. "Give these birds sweet dreams!"

Terra nodded, digging into her kit. "What does Marina say: I got it? I made it?" She pulled two large bottles from the kit. "I found it!" She uncorked the bottles. "I think I need a better battle cry than that."

"I hope you're not going to help those creatures!" Dav'yn cried, slashing his knife through the air at the G'unk-g'unks.

"No …"

"Good!"

"Now get away, Dav'yn!"

"I will not!"

"This stuff is strong!"

"You're going to HEAL them!"

"I'm warning you —"

Terra mixed the two liquids and tossed the mixture into the air. She quickly turned away, shutting her eyes and covering her face.

Dav'yn did not.

The liquid burst into a cloud.

He dropped like a rock to the ground.

As did the three G'unk-g'unks. The biggest one fell on top of Dav'yn.

Terra was about to help free Dav'yn, but she heard Xalid calling to her.

"Help! Terra!"

Terra gathered her kit and ran, dodging through the G'unk-g'unks, which pecked at her.

"Where's Marina when you need her?" she said. "I'm a healer, not a bird-watcher!"

Xalid was on the ground. His head was bleeding. Two G'unk-g'unks took turns swinging their massive heads down and pecking at him.

Terra used her kit as a shield and knocked one of the birds in the face. The bird recoiled not from the slap but from the odd noise of glass bottles rattling in the kit. It seemed to fear the sound.

Terra helped Xalid move under a cart. She dug into her kit and produced a soft white cloth, which she pressed to his head wound.

"Hold this," she said to Xalid. "I have birds to chase!"

She jumped out from under the cart, raised her kit and

shook it. The bottles clattered.

"Hah!" she said.

The birds paused and tilted their heads in unison, as if curious.

"Hah!" Terra said. "Fear my — medical kit!"

One of the birds leaned, flicked its beak and sent the kit flying out of her hands.

"Hah!" she said. "Fear my empty hands!" She moved her flat open palms in two small circles, wiggling her twelve fingers.

The G'unk-g'unks lunged at her.

Terra dodged. "Fear my running feet!"

She turned and sped away from them. She dashed past the caravan to witness an impossible sight: Lynai'seth, riding a G'unk-g'unk.

"So THAT'S what we're supposed to do!" Terra said. "Nobody told me!"

The G'unk-g'unk reared, swung Lynai'seth again and again into rock walls, lurched and twisted and flapped but failed to knock her off its back.

Gradually, the G'unk-g'unk grew tired.

S'yen screeched with pleasure. He took rope from Zwyna, lassoed another G'unk-g'unk and jumped on its back as Lynai'seth had. Ru'an followed.

The three of them struggled on the backs of the giant birds, but S'yen was able to lead his G'unk-g'unk towards the fencing that the others had constructed. As he and the giant bird passed into the enclosure, Lhista T'an slammed shut the gate she had made. Mohir'a'qest slipped a rope over the posts to secure them.

The Outcasts had trapped their first G'unk-g'unk.

Lynai'seth followed. S'yen jumped off his G'unk-g'unk, slipped off his Battle Gloves and applauded her. He helped guide the creature into the enclosure.

Ru'an followed on a G'unk-g'unk. Eventually, Gyro, Ignis and several other Outcasts were able to jump onto the beasts and steer them into the fencing.

Near the fallen carts, the giant birds regrouped. Some continued to peck, but many of them started running off in their original southwestern direction.

"We need to catch more of them!" Gyro shouted.

Terra joined Lynai'seth in the enclosure. Lynai'seth was leaning on a post, catching her breath, her wet hair cascading down her shoulders.

"You all right?" Terra asked.

Lynai'seth nodded.

"Do you often tame giant wild birds in the Shi'vaal Community?"

Lynai'seth shook her head. "First time."

"You're my new hero."

Lynai'seth looked at her. Her pupils were their normal color again. "Jax would have done the same thing." She took a deep breath, released and joined S'yen, Gyro, Ignis and the others as they tried capturing more G'unk-g'unks. She took rope from Mohir'a'qest, who beamed.

"I helped Lady Lynai'seth! I gave her rope! She's using my rope!"

"I helped everyone else," Zwyna said, jealousy in her voice.

The children circled and shouted and waved their hands.

All told, the Outcasts captured twenty-seven G'unk-g'unks. The fencing held fast despite the G'unk-g'unks' repeated efforts to break free.

They found one G'unk-g'unk that had lost its life in the battle.

Terra found Oolo, who had fainted.

Terra found Yan, who avoided all fighting and was furiously chronicling the battle in his book.

And Terra found Dav'yn, still asleep from the knockout potion she had tossed in the air. An equally sleeping G'unk-g'unk still lay atop of him in a feathery heap.

Chapter 12

The afternoon sun burned off the fog as if gently lifting a gray veil from sullen earth. As the veil of fog vanished, magnificent walls of rock appeared. The many strata of rock wavered in layers of deep brown, sand, turquoise, blood red and mossy green, serving as a living history of Dulunae. Yan had read the rings of a fallen tree to determine how many Sun Cycles it had existed. Now, he could study the strata of the wall and learn about the planet itself.

Gyro searched with Terra for a place to pitch camp. Dav'yn had recovered from Terra's knockout potion and followed them, offering hundreds of opinions.

S'yen and Ru'an were in the G'unk-g'unk pen. "*Abette!*" S'yen cried with glee, trying to stop a G'unk-g'unk from playfully pecking at him. "*Abette!*" He and Ru'an had spent the day taming the G'unk-g'unks. When they saw Lynai'seth step into the pen, Ru'an stopped, picked up a glistening green feather, dusted it off and handed it to her. Lynai'seth smiled appreciatively and slid the feather into her hair. Ru'an applauded.

"*Quar, Skrytesse!*" S'yen said. His broad smile and bright eyes indicated that the statement was a compliment.

Lynai'seth had been teaching Ru'an the Common Tongue and was able to talk with her. "How is everything?"

"Everything is good!" Ru'an said. She was feeling proud and important as she worked with S'yen. "The G'unk-g'unks are smart. And fast. They knocked me down forty-three times."

Lynai'seth gazed at the G'unk-g'unk leader. It had yet to

be tamed. Its black eyes squinted with suspicion. The bird honked and snorted as S'yen approached. He backed away.

Lynai'seth stepped forward cautiously, her hands raised, palms open in a peaceful gesture. She listened to the sounds of the G'unk-g'unks and sang a few notes. The flock of G'unk-g'unks stopped in their tracks and reared their heads in surprise.

"I hope this works." Lynai'seth sang again. Unlike the bright, high-pitched melodies she sang to calm the children, her conversation with the G'unk-g'unks was a repetition of low tones coupled with three high shrieks.

"*Shiya!*" S'yen said in awe.

"*Chee!*" Ru'an cried with delight.

Lynai'seth took the little girl's hand. "Let's see how well we do together." They stepped slowly, carefully towards the G'unk-g'unk leader. It watched them.

"How do you say 'be calm' in your language?" Lynai'seth asked.

"*Abette,*" Ru'an said. "It means to calm down, be easy and stop."

"Sing the word with me — quietly and calmly — as we approach the G'unk-g'unk leader. We'll show him respect."

They sang "*abette,*" starting low on the first syllable, raising the second syllable in higher tone. The bird watched.

S'yen was motionless but ready to strike in case the bird attacked them.

Lynai'seth gently lifted Ru'an and placed her on the back of the G'unk-g'unk. The bird continued to watch but did not buck or fight. Ru'an slowly slid a makeshift harness over its head and neck so that she could use a guiding rope without choking the animal. Lynai'seth took the reins and led Ru'an around the pen on the back of the G'unk-g'unk leader.

"*Shiya,*" S'yen said quietly.

Ru'an petted the animal, sang to it, smiled and laughed. The other birds watched as their leader gave the girl a ride.

"They're not bad," Ru'an explained. "They fight only when they're attacked."

Lynai'seth loosened her grip on the reins as they circled the pen. "What does your religion say we should do with the dead G'unk-g'unk?"

"Many things. First we wish its soul good journey to the Better Life. S'yen and I already did that. You can cook the meat and eat it. We won't, but we won't stop you. It's okay. We make tools from the bones and feathers. The insides offer many medicines. Nothing is left to waste. It would insult the G'unk-g'unk to leave any part of it to waste."

"I'll tell Gyro about the meat and Terra about the medicine."

"I wish Jax was here," Ru'an said. "He would be so happy seeing us with the G'unk-g'unk. He would be happy seeing you smile. He loves you so. All the children know it."

For once, Lynai'seth was caught speechless. She smiled faintly, then frowned, then saddened.

"Don't worry," Ru'an said. "He's still alive."

"How do you know?" Lynai'seth wondered.

"If a person passes to the Better Life, the Black Bird of Death rises, then bursts into flame in the sky to celebrate. I haven't seen the Black Bird."

"Then maybe he and Marina are still alive."

"Yes. S'yen is worried, though. It's the wrong time of the Sun Cycle for the G'unk-g'unks to migrate. Completely wrong. They were running from something. They're gentle but also very strong and brave. Nothing much frightens them."

"I know," Lynai'seth said, rubbing her sore neck. "This leader swung me into rock walls to prove its bravery and strength. What do you think *could* have scared them?"

Ru'an thought. "Antibodies and Shadow Beasts."

* * *

Spirits were high during the Council meeting at the fire that night. Gyro had found open pockets in the cliffs ideal for pitching camp. The Outcasts rolled the carts up a rocky incline, then unloaded food and supplies. They were away from the trail the G'unk-g'unks had used. They were protected from wind and rain. They could watch as any predators approached and keep a watchful eye on the G'unk-g'unk pen.

S'yen had prepared a meat feast from the dead G'unk-g'unk. Pots bubbled over the open fires as the rich meat stewed in its own juices. He sliced some withered potatoes and onions and dropped them into the pots. He dripped some of the animal's blood into the pots. When the stew was ready, he carefully poured it into bowls, not spilling a drop. Everyone dipped stale bread into the juices and greedily ate.

As S'yen approached Lynai'seth with a special bowl of the stew, he dropped to one knee in honor. "*Krytesse,*" he said, which Ru'an translated as "princess." He said in Avian language that he would always honor her courage and skill. Lynai'seth nodded.

S'yen gave Ignis some of the teeth of the bird. Ignis discovered that he could strike the teeth against rock to make sparks. And where there were sparks, he could create a healthy fire. He quickly discovered that if he struck the teeth in certain ways on the rock, he could create white, bright green, red, blue, myriad colors of sparks. The children applauded the display.

Lhista T'an and brother Tu'ghee T'an gathered the feathers. They used tiny G'unk-g'unk bones with eyelets as sewing needles. They cheerfully fashioned small pillows for the children and sewed a large blanket. The feathers would offer soft rest to the head and warmth to the body on cold nights.

S'yen gave Yan a feather to use as a writing quill and G'unk-g'unk blood to use as ink for his chronicles. Yan began drawing pictures of the flock of G'unk-g'unks. Dav'yn watched with interest.

With Ru'an translating, Terra struggled to understand everything S'yen was saying about the bird's skeleton, organs, veins, flesh, blood and muscles. It appeared that the bird's body could be used to cure almost everything from headaches to eye injuries, mouth sores, heart and stomach pains, sore muscles, flesh wounds and burns. Terra's eyes seemed as bright as the campfire as she studied the bird's carcass, took samples under S'yen's guidance and made detailed notes in her medical journal.

"I'll be able to do so much more to help everyone," Terra said. "The healers of my community would be jealous of this. Thank you so much."

Ru'an translated her comments to S'yen, who bowed to her.

"My friends," Gyro said, merriment in his voice, "this is a day to remember. For the first time, we acted as a group. We cooperated. As S'yen had asked, we gathered but did not harm the G'unk-g'unks. S'yen hopes to tame them so that they can help pull our carts. This means we can move farther and faster. This means that instead of pulling carts ourselves, we can *ride* in them."

The Outcasts cheered.

"Yes," Dav'yn said, wiping stew from his bowl with a piece of bread, "this is all well and good — for the moment. What of the future? You've lost your scouts — Master Marina and the other weak one. We face sudden death. Surely we won't stay here forever, waiting for brutal attacks on us during the night?"

"You can stand guard," Gyro said.

"What?"

"You worry about our safety. Make a plan. Guard us during the night."

"I am an advisor, not a sentry. I need sleep to strengthen my brain."

"Then I recommend you get plenty of sleep," Terra advised.

Gyro smiled. "I am proud of everyone," he said. "Proud of the efforts each of you made to serve the group. This has been my dream, and today I saw that dream come true. Tomorrow, I need helpers to fix the carts so we can sit on top of them. I need helpers to learn how to ride the G'unk-g'unks."

Outcasts raised their hands. "I'll help! I'll help!" they cried. Mohir'a'qest and Zwyna got into a contest of seeing who could raise a hand the highest.

"You need guides," Dav'yn snarled. "This childish celebration gets us nowhere. The scribe must teach me his language so we can plot a course." He gestured to Yan, who ignored him while he wrote.

"I'll observe him in silence," Dav'yn said.

"I would like to thank S'yen, Ru'an and Lynai'seth for capturing the G'unk-g'unks," Gyro said. "They acted bravely."

Outcasts applauded.

Lynai'seth bowed. "Thank you. I acted in memory of Jax. And Marina."

S'yen nodded to Ru'an and stood. "We're going to sleep by the pen," Ru'an explained. "S'yen knows how to keep the G'unk-g'unks calm during the night. They used to roam freely in our community. They were our pets before Antibodies came … and …" Her voice caught at the mention of her homeland. She sobbed.

Klanga stood. She crossed to Ru'an and extended Feelie to her. "Here," she said. "Feelie will keep you safe tonight."

The little ball of orange fur looked up at Ru'an with gleaming eyes. It purred softly as Ru'an took the creature into her arms. "Thank you," Ru'an said.

"That was very kind," Terra told Klanga.

"It's scary down there," Klanga said. "She needs all the help she can get."

S'yen armed himself with a knife, a bow, some arrows and his Battle Gloves with curving claws. Ru'an tucked a slingshot in her belt that Mohir'a'qest had made from sturdy wood. She put some smooth stones in a pouch and tied it to her belt. She then took Feelie in her arms and held the creature closely.

"Be careful," Klanga said.

Ru'an smiled. She enjoyed having Klanga fuss over her. She especially enjoyed acting like one of the older Outcasts. "I will," she said bravely.

"Feelie stays awake at night and watches out for monsters. If you fall asleep, Feelie will wake you up."

"I'm glad. But I don't think I'll be sleeping very much."

Klanga ran loving fingers through Feelie's bright fur. She leaned and kissed the animal. "You take care of Ru'an," she said. "She's my friend. Don't let anyone hurt her."

Feelie made a squeaking sound, as if to reassure Klanga.

Gyro used sign language with S'yen, telling him to whistle if there was any trouble. S'yen nodded.

"Dav'yn?" Gyro said. "Care to join them?"

Dav'yn looked up from Yan's book. "I'm sure that Bird Boy and Bird Girl can handle everything that comes their way."

The Outcasts stood and watched as S'yen and Ru'an marched down the rocky incline to the ground. They turned back, waved and headed off into the darkness. The Outcasts could hear the distinct *"gunk-gunk"* sound the birds were making in the pen.

Terra turned to Gyro and spoke in a low voice. "Do we have a plan in case Antibodies attack?"

Gyro grinned. "We always have a plan."

"It's good to see you smiling again. For a while, I thought we lost you."

Gyro paused. "Me, too."

He rejoined the group and helped the children prepare for sleep. They were able to walk into large pockets in the cave wall and place their mats on the ground. Ignis prepared small fires for each encampment. Some of the children made playful, wiggling shadows on the walls with their fingers and hands. Their young laughter echoed.

Lynai'seth settled the children, then stepped outside on a ledge. She tucked her arms into her sleeves and gazed in a northeastern direction.

Terra joined her. "That was some fancy bird riding you did today."

"I find myself doing things I've never done before."

They both gazed northeast, in the direction of the crystal caves.

"They're coming back," Terra said.

Lynai'seth sighed. "I'm not so sure. Even if Jax and Marina have survived, they'll never catch up with us. Especially with the animals pulling our carts."

"Marina is an expert tracker. We've left enough footprints for an army to find us."

Lynai'seth looked at her.

"I was joking," Terra said. "Tell me something — how do you feel about Jax?"

"I ... I ..."

"I thought so."

"There is no love in our Shi'vaal Community, if that's what you're thinking," Lynai'seth said. "Especially between my community and Jax's Kerta Community. I wasn't even able to speak to him for the longest time."

"At first, you didn't talk to *anyone.*"

"I had to observe the Silence with everyone but the children. It's the way I was raised. There is only purpose with the Shi'vaal, not love. We are taught that from birth. Since the Antibodies have destroyed everything, there doesn't seem to be any purpose anywhere."

"Everyone finds purpose in how you handle the children. You keep their spirits alive."

"I'm tired," Lynai'seth admitted.

"You've had a busy day. And you haven't been sleeping well. None of us has. I think we will tonight, though, after that stew. Try to get some rest. Healer's orders."

Terra left.

Lynai'seth pulled a sword from the shadows. It was one of the few family artifacts she had rescued from the Antibody attack on her community. She had let Jax use the sword — her mother's sword — in a fight against Shadow Beasts.

The sword was lightweight. When she slashed it through the air, it sang a single high note.

Lynai'seth looked closely at the weapon. It bore the same markings on the hilt and blade as on the cuffs and hem of her dress.

She whispered something. Her soft words slid on the wind, into darkness.

The wind lifted, and clouds rolled through the night sky.

Lynai'seth slowly raised the sword, then flicked her wrist. The metal sang. She swung it again and again. The sword cried to the night in anguish, in a pain beyond all human expression.

She swung it again and again, in front of her, over her head, her hair falling loose and brow sweating. Finally, Lynai'seth brought the blade crashing down on jutting rock. There was an explosion of sparks, a loud clang. The sword sliced the rock from its ancient anchoring.

In the sky, the clouds pulsed with white light, and the rains came.

Lynai'seth swung the sword as if trying to stop the rain, to bat away the clouds. No use. Lightning pulsed. Thunder rolled moments after the flash in the sky. Rain fell in darts.

She heard the collective cry of the G'unk-g'unks. Before running down to help S'yen and Ru'an, she noticed something to the northeast.

A pair of eyes.

A body, low to the ground.

She could see it when lightning flashed. The figure disappeared in the darkness.

Lightning flashed, and the creature reappeared.

Then it was gone.

Lynai'seth's slight smile faded. It wasn't Jax. Or Marina.

The creature had a milky white form, but it wasn't an Antibody.

Wasn't a Shadow Beast.

In a final flash of lightning, Lynai'seth looked below her at something new. In the light, she could see through its flesh and fur, right to its bones. The creature moved with steady purpose, as if stalking something.

Then the light vanished.

Chapter 13

Sword in hand, Lynai'seth ran down the rain-spattered rock, past the carts, to the G'unk-g'unk pen. The birds were shifting fitfully in the downpour.

"S'yen!" she called. "Ru'an!"

Thunder muttered in the night.

"S'yen!"

"Lynai'seth!" Ru'an finally replied.

Lynai'seth circled the pen and found S'yen setting up a row of clay pots. "Hi!" Ru'an called out, her wet hair matted to her face. She was holding Feelie tightly.

"Everything all right?"

"Of course!" Ru'an said. "The G'unk-g'unks aren't afraid of rain. They like it. Look!"

The birds were tilting their heads back, drinking raindrops.

"We're collecting extra rainwater in the pots," Ru'an said. "Are you okay? Why are you here?"

Lynai'seth paused. She saw a white figure in the distance. "I — wanted to make sure you were safe," she said.

"We're fine, thank you. You can go back to the children," Ru'an said, as if she were no longer one of them. "They're probably scared, and they need you."

S'yen bowed to Lynai'seth. His thick, tangled hair hung like wet feathers on his head. He had never looked happier.

Lynai'seth saw something out of the corner of her eye. She left.

Instead of returning to the camp, she followed the trail of the mysterious creature. She had feared it would attack Ru'an and S'yen, or perhaps the G'unk-g'unks. It was circling the pen but keeping its distance.

Lynai'seth kept a steady hand on her sword as she drew near it. She veered to the left, hid behind a rock, waited and watched.

Lightning flashed. The creature was suddenly far to the right of her.

She followed, keeping a safe distance.

Another snake-tongue lick of lightning across the sky.

Now the creature was far ahead, to her left.

It looked as if it had turned its head to wait for her.

Lynai'seth crept along rain-drenched rock, past crags, under dripping ledges.

Darkness and light, darkness and light. Silver pools of water on the ground — like stepping stones to a fantastic, unknown place.

A pounding of clouds above.

Lightning bolts.

The world alive with electric menace.

The creature disappeared, then reappeared, as if it were a streak of lightning dancing along the ground.

Lynai'seth walked into a series of narrow rocky passages. She paused. She could still turn around and go back to camp instead of wandering off into the unknown. This was exactly how the Outcasts had lost Jax and Marina.

She poked her sword into the darkness.

Something — a low moan.

Growling.

Somehow the creature had ducked behind her. She swung her sword backward to protect herself.

The creature kept its distance.

Lightning seemed to snap like a blanket, first everywhere, then nowhere.

"Show yourself!" Lynai'seth shouted.

The creature ignored the command.

"Coward!"

In a blink, the creature was above her, on a slick ledge. She could see two white eyes, a coiling tongue, milky white body and curving bones of a rib cage.

She could see teeth — two jagged rows, each tooth as long as her index finger.

All at once the sky burst with light and the creature jumped. Lynai'seth stepped backwards and slipped on slick rock. She fell. The creature was falling like a crushing rock upon her. Lynai'seth ran the sword up into the air to protect herself.

The creature was gone.

She scrambled to her feet. Her long hair felt like heavy rope around her. Her dress weighed her down. The rain blinded her.

The creature appeared like a thought.

Lynai'seth reacted with sharp reflexes, her sword jabbing the night. The tip scraped along rock.

The creature bounded behind her again.

This time, Lynai'seth stood and took the offense. Rather than wait for the creature's next move, she swung the sword back and forth until it sang a song of pain for the creature. Whether she struck it or not, Lynai'seth carved a path for herself out of the rocky passages.

"Heeyah!" she shouted. "Heeyah!"

Her arm swept with blinding speed. She moved from the narrow rock to the open trail, back to the G'unk-g'unk pen. The white creature kept its distance.

She glanced — S'yen and Ru'an were in the pen, offering bowls of captured rainwater to the huge birds. The animals seemed to rejoice in the rainfall, their throaty voices clear and resonant.

Lynai'seth stopped. She looked around in a circle.

The creature was nowhere to be found.

"Have you seen anything?" she called to Ru'an.

"Only the G'unk-g'unks!" the girl answered.

Lynai'seth slowly, cautiously returned to the rocky incline that led to the Outcast camp. She couldn't see anything following her. She climbed to the top of the incline — still no creature.

Lynai'seth stood looking over the landscape. The storm had passed as quickly as it had struck, sweeping to other dark destinations. The clouds parted, revealing a twinkling of stars and the twin moons, remote and aloof, their white eyes nearly shut.

She stood guard, sword at the ready. Some of the Outcasts had set out large casks and bowls to collect rainwater as S'yen and Ru'an had in the bird pen.

Gyro crossed to her. "Lynai'seth! We've been looking for you! The children have been crying. We just can't calm them as easily as you can."

"I saw ..." She looked below at the silver puddles of rainwater.

"Saw what?"

"Thought I saw —"

"What? Antibodies?"

"No —"

"More Shadow Beasts?"

"No."

"Great. Something new?"

"I don't know what I saw," Lynai'seth admitted.

"Maybe a trick of the light."

"Maybe." Lynai'seth turned to Gyro. "I'll check on the children."

"Thank you. Every time Dav'yn walks by in the night, the children scream."

Lynai'seth crossed to the cliff dwelling where the children sat huddled in a corner. Ignis had lit a low fire to ease their fears.

"Rain!" a child cried.

"Lightning!" another one shouted.

"Thunder!"

"Monsters!"

"There are no monsters in here," Lynai'seth said. "Only your fears. Now go back to sleep. Lie down and I'll sing a song."

"What kind of song?"

"The same kind my mother sang to me when I was your age and afraid of the rain."

"You aren't afraid of anything!"

"Oh, yes, I am." Lynai'seth took a deep breath, released, breathed in again and sang a light song that wove through the fire, the shadows and the quick breath of the panicked children. The tune was slow and soothing. The children

yawned and returned to their mats and fell asleep.

When the last child passed into sleep, Lynai'seth stepped out onto a ledge. She found a rock to lean on. She slid to the ground and rested the sword on her lap.

The night had the clarity of polished crystal. The stars spoke their tales of ancient Cycles, lost histories, and distant worlds, if such things existed. The stars formed bows and arrows, long, curving blades, fish, horses, birds, a pageant of splendor.

Lynai'seth watched for the white creature. She watched until she could look no more, until the weight of sleep finally bore down and overtook her.

The twin moons moved through the clear night sky as if searching for something precious and lost.

The Outcasts settled, and slept.

The sun slowly rose, transforming a dull, dusty predawn sky into a startling sweep of pink, like millions of flowers suddenly cast to the light.

Lynai'seth's eyes were shut. Her sword glistened as the sun rose.

Somewhere, not far away, deep black eyes peered at her.

Not far away, the white creature stood, its intent as unknown as the night.

Chapter 14

Like a wilted flower, Lynai'seth turned to the morning light and felt renewed. Her long hair had dried and was thick and wavy. Her soft purple skin glowed like an amethyst gemstone. The sword on her lap shone in gold and silver hues. Her dress was dry and amazingly clean, the mud crumbling in bits and falling to the ground.

For a few sleepy moments, she kept her eyes shut. A cool breeze stroked her face. She smiled, dimples appearing at the corners of her mouth.

"Sleep well?" a voice asked her.

"Jax," she said.

"Hardly."

Lynai'seth opened her eyes. Terra handed her a bowl of stew left over from the night before. "Gyro says you had an adventure last night," Terra said.

Lynai'seth looked at the ground. "I thought I saw something — a white creature. Stalking."

"I asked — no one else saw anything. Not even Dav'yn, who views the entire world as unusual."

"It moved with the lightning. I thought it might attack Ru'an and S'yen. Or maybe the G'unk-g'unks."

"I just visited S'yen. Nothing bad happened overnight. The birds drank rainwater and seemed tame this morning. Ru'an says she and S'yen want to start training us to ride the birds and hitch them to the carts."

Lynai'seth placed her sword on the ground, stood and stretched. She stopped. "The rain."

"What about it?"

"It washed our footprints away. Jax and Marina will never find us now."

"I was hoping they would have caught up with us last night. Maybe ..." Terra's voice trailed off.

"Maybe what?" Lynai'seth demanded.

"Maybe — we need to start believing that they're not coming back."

"They are! Ru'an says that in the Avian Community, the Black Bird of Death appears when a person loses his life."

"Then — maybe that's what you saw last night. The Black Bird of Death."

"It was white!"

"In flashes of lightning, *everything* looks white."

"No —" Lynai'seth clutched a hand to her collar. "No. Haven't you had any more visions like you did the other night?"

"I tried," Terra said. "Nothing. I couldn't feel a thing. Only a cold emptiness."

"I refuse to believe they're gone. Maybe I should go back and look for them."

"You can't get back into the crystal caves. The passage is sealed shut with rock."

"There have to be other passages."

"Maybe. Maybe not. We can't afford to lose you. We have to keep moving ahead."

"Moving ahead to what?" Lynai'seth asked.

"HayVen. You know that."

"Truth be told, the people of my community have never heard of such a place."

"Frankly," Terra said, "neither have mine. Then again, we never heard of G'unk-g'unks, either, and the area is crawling with them. So who knows? Now come on — eat some stew and join us in the pen."

Terra left. Lynai'seth ate the stew. She stood watch over the trail for a while. The cliffs cast deep, jagged shadows on the ground. The rain had, indeed, washed away all footprints.

She stared northeast. A dot appeared in the distant sky. The dot swelled, took shape. It was a V-formation of birds.

Black birds.

They flew directly at her and shot like a single black arrow overhead, carving the morning light with their frantic flight, then disappearing in the southwestern sky.

Lynai'seth blinked away tears.

She was about to turn away and join the Outcasts when something below caught her eye. It looked as if a strange, transparent liquid had moved into the light just past the edge of a cliff shadow. In another trick of morning light, the liquid looked like an animal.

Like the white creature she had seen during the night!

It appeared, then seemed to quickly blend into light. She couldn't keep watch on it. It was invisible, then milky white, then invisible again.

She took up her sword and stepped carefully down to the trail. She swung the blade behind her.

Nothing.

She moved forward, slowly and cautiously.

Ahead, Outcasts had climbed atop G'unk-g'unks in the pen. The birds were actually quite friendly, allowing the strange, featherless, two-legged beings to climb atop them for a ride. The G'unk-g'unks straightened their necks and stiffened their bodies so the riders would not fall off. S'yen rode the G'unk-g'unk leader. Ru'an followed on another bird. The birds pranced about in proud display.

Gyro mounted an animal, as did Ignis, Lhista T'an, Tu'ghee T'an, Terra and Xalid. Zwyna and Mohir'a'qest struggled to see who could climb a G'unk-g'unk the quickest. Zu-thenn, who had been seriously injured by an Antibody, watched with Oolo. Oolo snatched a bug from the air and put it in his mouth.

Klanga had retrieved Feelie from Ru'an. She placed Feelie on the back of a bird, and the little orange creature rode with confidence atop the G'unk-g'unk.

Dav'yn kept his distance. As Lynai'seth approached, he spoke to her. "These creatures are meant for eating, not riding."

Lynai'seth kept a watchful eye behind her. "Are you afraid to ride one?"

"Afraid? *Mephiste!* I am afraid of wasting time and energy. Why do you brandish your sword? Have you come to kill one for our dinner tonight, perhaps? You are wise."

"I come to protect."

"Maybe you'll join me in convincing everyone to head southeast, not southwest. That way lies ruin."

"How do you know?"

"I can read the rocks! The trails! The sky! The wind itself! The earth trembles. Birds flee. I'm sure the rhyming Bug Boy would say that even insects are taking flight. The road southwest is short-lived. The passage southeast leads to safety."

"If that's true, why haven't you gone southeast without us?"

"I can put everyone's skills to their best use. We can build a new Community, not waste time seeking a fabled 'HayVen.' Do you believe such a place exists?"

"No."

"Then why do you follow that self-appointed leader? He takes us from one danger to the next. He let Master Marina and your — *friend* — the Round Head die in the caves without a search for them. His moods shift. His skin is a rainbow of colors, revealing these shifting moods. I don't ask to be leader — I seek only cooperation until we regain our own footing. After we build our new Community, we'll scout for other survivors. We'll create a library of information so that our cultures stay alive. My Infernal Community has a simple motto: Spare Yourself. That is what I intend to do. Will you consider my words?"

Lynai'seth paused. "Yes."

Dav'yn smiled, his canine teeth appearing. "That's all I ask."

Ru'an walked a G'unk-g'unk to Lynai'seth. "Come on!"

"Let me have the honor of holding your weapon," Dav'yn said.

Lynai'seth thought a moment, then handed the sword to him. She climbed the back of the G'unk-g'unk. The creature made its throaty sound. Lynai'seth took the reins, clicked her tongue and tapped her legs on its side. The G'unk-g'unk marched around the pen.

"They're good!" Ru'an said. "They'll help us!"

Lynai'seth joined Gyro, Terra, Xalid and S'yen as they rode

G'unk-g'unks. S'yen led a dance that involved all five of them weaving back and forth. He demonstrated how a G'unk-g'unk could run swiftly and stop quickly without throwing its rider.

Terra waved. "S'yen says that G'unk-g'unk waste can be used as a skin oil and insect repellant. Isn't that great?"

Gyro laughed. "I'm glad you can get excited about something like that. Any volunteers for a clean-up team?"

The children laughed and pointed to one another.

Lhista T'an handed little Kg to Lynai'seth. The boy sat wide-eyed as she slowly guided the G'unk-g'unk around the pen. When they stopped, he clapped his hands excitedly.

"He likes it!" Ru'an said.

The Outcasts quickly learned how to handle the animals. Gyro ordered the Outcasts to strike camp, load the carts and pull them to the G'unk-g'unk pen. S'yen and Xalid slid harnesses around the birds, then adjusted the carts. Each cart had two birds to pull it. Tu'ghee T'an and Lhista T'an had rigged crates on which the cart drivers could sit and steer the G'unk-g'unks. When the last carts were readied, they worked with Zwyna and Mohir'a'qest to untie the pen and pull up the fence posts and gate. They worked as a team, racing and laughing.

Lynai'seth retrieved her sword from Dav'yn. "A fine piece of weaponry," he said. "A little too light for me, though."

"Hold out your hand."

"Never! Why?"

"Show your courage."

"My courage is the silent kind."

"Hold out your hand."

Lynai'seth stepped back. Dav'yn tentatively held out his hand. Before another breath, Lynai'seth whipped the sword through the air.

"AHH!" Dav'yn cried.

The sword sliced through a piece of rope Dav'yn had tied around his wrist. The rope fell to the ground. His skin was untouched — not a scratch.

"My sword is light but accurate," she said. Then walked away.

"You'll make someone a fine mate someday!" he called after her, studying his wrist.

Lynai'seth stepped from the pen. She looked for the mysterious creature but could not see it. She joined the children by their carts, placing her sword in the bed of a cart near her sleeping mat.

The Outcasts organized themselves in a long row of carts. Gyro gave instructions to everyone, then led the way in his cart. He whistled and snapped the reins. The two G'unk-g'unks lurched forward. The cart jolted, then rolled after them. Each cart followed.

The children laughed. Older Outcasts had pulled them in their carts across the rugged terrain at an achingly slow rate. The G'unk-g'unks moved quickly. The children felt exhilarated, as if on holiday from a merciless school. They had eaten well the night before, had rested, had drunk fresh rainwater and now rode under the power of giant, brightly colored birds. This was the stuff of fairy tales, come to life.

Lynai'seth looked back, for a sign of the creature, for a sign of Jax, Marina, for any sign of life that might pursue them.

There was nothing.

There was the wash of bright sunlight, the black quilting of shadows, the rainbow strata of rock.

There was the camp, left behind. There was the crystal cave, left farther behind. There was the presence of Marina and Jax, left to the dark fates of the deep underground world, buried beyond sight.

Only after the Outcasts moved far along the trail did the white creature emerge from its invisible realm into the light of day.

Chapter 15

Time passed in slow, steady cadence. Sunlight poured like honey down the rocky walls. Low trees with brush as tight as fists appeared, dotting the dusty countryside.

After a while, Gyro was able to loosen his reins. The G'unk-g'unks knew where to walk, how quickly to set the pace and when to rest. S'yen said, through Ru'an's translation, that the birds would follow the trail of the original flock of G'unk-g'unks that had migrated past them.

The Outcasts delighted at the speed of progress. They had spent so long walking, almost crawling across hostile landscapes, hiding in caves or cliff dwellings. Now they could ride in the open air. The trials of the journey had now brightened into adventure.

At one point, the G'unk-g'unks veered southeast.

"At last!" Dav'yn cried.

S'yen gestured to let the birds follow their instincts. The birds led them to a small series of murky brown pools. The pooling water floated into a narrow creek. The creek, in turn, opened to a deep purple stream. The low trees offered cooling shade.

The G'unk-g'unks lined up side-by-side along the stream. S'yen held up his hand, suggesting that everyone let the birds proceed with whatever it was they had planned. Ru'an smiled.

"What's going on?" Lynai'seth whispered to her.

"You'll see."

The G'unk-g'unks leaned closely to the water, then dunked their heads into it.

And didn't come up for air.

"They're drowning!" Klanga cried.

"Save them!" a boy shouted.

"Drowning!"

"G'unk-g'unks! NO!"

"Stop!"

S'yen kept his hand raised.

"I've seen animals do this in desperation," Dav'yn said. "They lose all hope."

Bubbles rose in the purple stream.

"Drowning!"

More bubbles.

"Please!"

Finally, one by one, the G'unk-g'unks lifted their massive heads from the water. Each bird had something trapped in its beak.

"Fish!" Gyro cried.

The G'unk-g'unks ate some of the fish whole, then spat others onto the ground. Outcasts jumped from their carts and grabbed for the wriggling fish. The G'unk-g'unks made repeated strikes into the water until they had eaten or gathered at least a hundred fish.

The Outcasts hurriedly tossed the fish into casks, bowls, anything they could find. Kg was sitting in the grass, trying to calm his trembling arms and legs. A fish fell next to him. He grabbed the fish in his small, rubbery hands. It spurted from his grip. Kg lunged for the fish. It escaped. The chase continued until Kg grabbed the fish a final time and slipped his fingers into its gills.

He held up the fish triumphantly.

The children cheered him.

"I believe Kg has caught us dinner," Gyro said.

Ignis wasted no time in creating small fires to cook the fish. He pulled fallen twigs and branches from the trees and arranged the kindling in a series of campfires. Outcasts used branches, stripped the bark, sharpened ends to a point and speared the fish. They then held the fish over the fires.

The Outcasts devoured their meal. Lhista T'an gathered the fish bones in a sack. To her, there was no such thing as waste. Everything ever created had a purpose. The trick was to find the right purpose.

The G'unk-g'unks seemed to doze while standing. They shut their eyes, satisfied from the bounty of the stream.

The Outcasts retreated to the shade of the trees. Some of them curled up on sweeps of tall grass and fell asleep.

Dav'yn watched as Gyro, Terra and Xalid checked the carts and bird harnesses for wear and tear.

Gyro patted Ru'an on the shoulder. "Tell S'yen that the G'unk-g'unks are a blessing for us."

"Oh, he knows," Ru'an said. "Birds are all precious. We have a lot to learn from them."

"What are they doing now?" Terra wondered.

Ru'an looked at the G'unk-g'unks gathered near a cluster of trees. "Some are resting. Others are eating. They find the right plants."

"The *right* plants? What are the wrong plants?"

"Poisonous."

"And they know the difference when they eat?

"Of course."

Terra smiled. "I think I should get to know them better."

"As do I," Dav'yn said. "My brain craves learning."

"You might as well start sometime," Terra said with a smile. She grabbed her kit and hurried off to the G'unk-g'unks. They were leaning to the ground and grazing on light yellow plants with long green stems. She watched as they lifted their heads, moved their beaks and slowly chewed the plants, then swallowed. Terra could almost see the chewed plants running down through their long throats.

The G'unk-g'unks roamed among a variety of wildflowers, some deep blue, others soft violet, bright red, soft yellow or orange with black dots. They ate only the yellow flowers.

Terra leaned and picked a few of the yellow plants. The giant birds ignored her. When she reached for the orange plants with black dots, a G'unk-g'unk leaned and slapped her hand with the bottom of its beak.

"Ow! Okay," Terra said, "I get the message. The black and orange plants are poisonous."

Dav'yn watched but kept his distance.

Terra sat cross-legged and picked yellow plants as G'unk-g'unks dipped their heads to the left and right of her. Occasionally a G'unk-g'unk would playfully nudge her with its beak.

Lynai'seth approached, sword at her side. Terra invited her to join them, but Lynai'seth seemed preoccupied with studying the stream. She passed by them without comment, then squatted by the water's edge. She held her sword across her knees and gazed down into the clear water flowing over smooth stones.

"She thinks she's better than everyone," Dav'yn said.

Terra looked at him. "Leave her alone. She takes care of

thirteen children all the time. How would *you* like to take care of them instead of her?"

Dav'yn shivered at the thought. "Children are the worst monsters imaginable."

"Weren't you a child once?"

"No. There was no time in my community for childhood."

"That's too bad."

"Too bad? It made us strong!"

"Dav'yn," Terra said, "it makes you sad."

"Bah!"

Suddenly, Lynai'seth grabbed her sword and stabbed it repeatedly into the water, making great splashes. The G'unk-g'unks reared back at the noise.

"She's gone mad!" Dav'yn said.

Terra jumped to her feet. "Maybe she's catching fish."

They hurried to Lynai'seth's side. "What is it?" Terra asked.

Lynai'seth stabbed the water again and again.

"What is it?"

Lynai'seth slashed the surface of the stream.

Terra shook her shoulder. "WHAT IS IT?"

Lynai'seth stopped. She was breathing heavily. Her long hair, though braided, hung loosely around her. "I saw —"

"What?"

"— saw a *face* in the water."

"Your reflection?"

"No! Something … the white creature …"

"The what?"

Lynai'seth squinted down at the water, which was slowly settling.

Minnows shot like small black darts past her.

Two stones lay like white eyes in the water. Light brown stones looked like teeth.

In a trick of light, the stream glistened like a mirror, revealing Lynai'seth's worried face. "Nothing," she finally said. "I saw nothing."

Terra leaned. "Maybe you should go rest with the children."

Lynai'seth turned to her. "Maybe I should."

Terra helped Lynai'seth stand. They crossed through the grass and headed for the trees where the children slept in the cool shade. Gyro crossed to them. Lynai'seth pointed to the stream, shook her hand, then lowered her head. Gyro cautiously took the sword from her.

While they stood in the distance, while the G'unk-g'unks wandered to other parts of the stream, while the other Outcasts were occupied and no one watched, Dav'yn squatted to the ground.

He reached for a handful of plants.

He tore the plants from the ground and quickly stuffed them into the pouch tied to his belt.

The plants were orange with black dots.

Not far away, the little boy named Kg sat in a patch of grass, rocking back and forth in the cool breeze. Something caught his attention. He stopped rocking. He watched as the tall red man reached for the orange plants with black dots, pulled them from the ground and jammed them into his pouch.

Kg opened his mouth to say something.

As usual, only warm breath, spit bubbles and strange gasping sounds issued from his lips.

Chapter 16

The Outcasts enjoyed food, water and a much-needed rest. The G'unk-g'unks ducked their heads into the stream to catch fish. They slept standing up.

The travellers enjoyed rare moments of peace.

The sun drifted, settled in the west. The sky unfurled in a vast veil of deep purple and blue. The sun looked like a magnificent jewel, ablaze in orange and white. Thick, billowy clouds were burnished in golden hues. The wind was cool and soothing.

"Is this HayVen?" Klanga asked Gyro. She stroked Feelie's soft fur.

Gyro's skin was as gold as the clouds. "No," he said with a faint smile. "HayVen is rich with flowers and trees and soft grass. Cool waters curl through the forests. People of all different communities walk together, smile. Sometimes they sing and dance. There's never any fear. Never any pain or punishment. No Antibodies. Rainbow birds glide through the sky. Clouds form, and soft rains fall to nourish the land. People live on and on, in true harmony, for more Sun Cycles than we can imagine."

"Do people die there?"

Gyro thought a moment. "Yes, but they're prepared. They pass peacefully, in old age."

"Where do they pass to?"

"I suppose it depends on what you believe. Some people believe there is Something Beyond HayVen, a place of immeasurable perfection."

"A place of what?"

"A place of nonsense," Dav'yn interrupted. "Why do you lie to this child? Why do you lead her to hope for something that doesn't exist? How cruel are you?"

"HayVen exists," Gyro said.

"How do you know?"

"I know."

"There are many among the group who doubt you."

"I'm sure. Anyone is free to leave at any time."

"And starve in the wilderness, or be eaten alive by *monstri umbrae*?"

"The Shadow Beasts have proven they can be allies. They helped us fight the last Antibody attack."

"The only thing they were doing was protecting themselves. They had no intention of rescuing us. I've seen them up close — they're brutal creatures. Blood-thirsty. And the longer we stay here, the better the chance they have for catching up with us."

"Are you referring to the Shadow Beasts or Marina and Jax?"

Dav'yn squinted. "I haven't given the Master and the Round Head a single thought. Most likely they are bones and dust by now."

Klanga's eyes filled with tears. "Do — you really think so?"

"Truth is truth."

"We don't give up hope on my watch," Gyro said. He knelt and put his large hands on Klanga's shoulders. "Never give up hope."

She sniffled. "I'll try not to."

"Your bedtime stories are so soothing for little minds," Dav'yn said.

Gyro rose. He stood a head taller than Dav'yn. He was heavier and stronger. His skin color deepened to the purple of the twilight sky. His eyes seemed to glow.

"Enough," was all he said.

Dav'yn smiled. "I'm a threat to you."

Gyro turned away from him. He took Klanga's hand and led her to the other children, who were gathered in a circle, listening to stories.

"You fear me because I tell the truth!" Dav'yn shouted after them. "I don't offer false promises about places that don't exist!"

Terra crossed to Dav'yn's side. "What are you shouting about? You're hurting my ears."

"He is dangerous," Dav'yn said.

"Who is dangerous?"

"The so-called leader. He drifts from place to place without regard for our lives."

"This place seems pretty nice."

"It's temporary. It's no place to make a home. We need to head southeast. Whip these animals until they carry us to safety."

"We need food and rest. As do the G'unk-g'unks."

"There is danger in the wind," Dav'yn said. "I can feel it. The earth trembles, rocks fall, animals race to safety."

"You need to drink some soothing tea."

"What?"

"Your stomach is in knots. I can feel it."

"Will you help me revolt?" Dav'yn asked.

"I don't know," Terra said. "You're pretty revolting on your own."

"Laugh tonight. Die tomorrow."

"That's a comforting thought."

"I've said enough."

"Now that's the smartest thing I've ever heard you say."

Terra almost tripped over Oolo, who was crawling across the ground on his hands and knees. "At least I need to find the feast."

"What are you babbling about this time?" Dav'yn asked.

"Food for thought is what I've sought. The birds ate them all. I feel small."

"He's hungry," Terra said. "The G'unk-g'unks ate all of the insects."

Dav'yn waved his hand as if Oolo were nothing more than a big, pesky insect himself. "Get away from here!"

Oolo looked up at him. "Away, you say?"

"Far, far away."

"I'm up the creek for food I seek?"

"Our Leader thinks the area is safe. Go anywhere you want. Crawl or stand tall."

Oolo smiled. "Crawl or stand tall?" He stood.

"I don't think it's a good idea to go too far," Terra said. "It's getting dark."

"Oolo will embark — before the dark!"

Dav'yn put a hand on his shoulder. "Go, and don't be slow." He shoved him.

Oolo stumbled but kept from falling. He wove a path through the camp and wandered upstream.

"That wasn't very bright," Terra said.

"Well," Dav'yn said, "he's young and dumb. I was surviving on my own at half his age."

"I mean it wasn't bright of you to send him off like that."

"What's wrong? Aren't we living in the Leader's dream world, safe and secure?"

"Not yet, we aren't."

Dav'yn glared at Terra. "So you doubt him?"

"I —"

Mohir'a'qest ran to Terra. He was out of breath. "We ... she ... I ..."

Terra grabbed his arm. "Slow down! What happened?"

"Zwyna ... we were seeing who could go in the water the farthest. She stepped, cut her foot, it's bleeding all over the place ..."

"Take me to her!"

Dav'yn leaned back and folded his arms. He watched Oolo disappear into the twilight shadows. He watched Terra rush to find Zwyna.

All the while, Kg watched him.

***

"Yes ... this is best ... put me to the test."

Oolo often talked aloud to himself. Not many of the others spoke with him or listened to his rhymes. No one seemed to like him.

He was a slim, awkward boy and often had a hard time walking from one place to another without injuring himself. As he crept from the Outcast camp, he snagged his pants on a thorny bush. Oolo pulled himself free, tearing the cloth.

"A rip on this trip."

Oolo moved along the edge of the water. His bony arms and legs pumped as if he were a fantastic insect in search of its home. Night shadows seemed to rise from the mud, blend with the bushes and trees and form a twilight wall impossible to escape.

He crawled on.

Something the size of his thumbnail flickered. A quick green blink of light. Oolo smiled.

"A light in the night, what a sight!"

Most of the Outcasts thought Oolo was strange. He had orange skin and large brown freckles — to some he looked like a diseased piece of fruit. He smiled often, revealing his brown, crooked teeth. He laughed at his own jokes in an odd way, as if gargling water in his throat and coughing it up through his nose. And, of course, he ate bugs. The Outcasts ate insects in tough times, to survive. Oolo found them a delicacy, a reason to wake up in the morning.

He knew the Common Tongue but chose to speak in short rhymes. Oolo had tried fighting Antibodies when they attacked his community. He failed. An Antibody repeatedly struck him in the head with a rock. Terra used the word 'traumatized' to describe him, a disturbed state of mind that kept Oolo hidden in his safe little world of rhymes.

Still, Oolo had helped Marina and Jax to look for Shadow Beasts. There was a flickering of courage deep in his heart.

"*Kee as'tarlyx*," he whispered with delight. The phrase from his community meant 'firefly of green light.'

The green light blinked, then vanished.

Oolo followed.

He tripped on tree roots, shrubs and rocks hidden in the night. He stumbled into a shallow hole. His bony arms were scratched and bruised. He was used to injuring himself, and he smiled.

"I hurt in the dirt."

The green light hovered over him. He swiped his arm through the air but missed the light.

Oolo worked his way to his feet. He was determined to catch the *kee as'tarlyx* and eat it. He wandered farther from the camp, deeper into the folds of night, the looming darkness, the hidden danger.

In a trick of light, he thought he saw paw-prints in the mud along the creek. They looked familiar. Not the prints of the G'unk-g'unks but —

Oolo smiled. "I don't fear it, in the least, this —"

He heard something — a soft, whining cry. The green light floated in the direction of the noise.

Oolo hurried. The creek seemed to disappear under a jagged ledge of rock. The light flew into the black hollow under the ledge. Oolo dropped to the ground and crawled, following the *kee as'tarlyx*.

The hollow led to a grotto, a series of tunnels and twisting routes in the rock. Oolo stood in an open area and wiped mud and grass from his clothing. As he did, the *kee as'tarlyx* flew near him. In a quick sweep of his hand, he grabbed the firefly and put it in his mouth. For a moment, the insect was still alive and his mouth glowed green.

The whining cry grew louder. Oolo, with mouth still lit green, leaned and looked.

He saw a nest.

In the nest sat three tiny animals, whining.

Oolo carefully approached.

Each creature was about the size of his palm. Each had soft, fuzzy fur.

Small red eyes.

Serpentine tails.

And five legs.

"Shh, shh, hush," Oolo said softly, "don't be in a rush." He moved closer to the nest. The tiny creatures didn't seem to notice him.

"You need to eat. I'll find a treat."

Another *kee as'tarlyx* floated through the air just above him. Oolo jumped to grab it so he could feed the little animals.

He tripped and fell on the nest.

The creatures squealed and ran.

In a blink, a monstrous animal jumped from one of the holes in the rocky wall and landed next to Oolo. Its eyes burned red as fire, its long green tongue licked the earth, its fur stood on end, its tail writhed with fury.

Oolo crawled backwards. "Friend?" he said weakly.

The creature snarled.

Oolo tried to stand and run. He tripped on a rock and fell into a ditch.

The fierce animal leapt through the air at him. Its jaw snapped open, then snapped shut. Its claws tore at his body.

Oolo screamed and screamed again.

His voice echoed in the dark canyon of rock.

Chapter 17

L ynai'seth!"

"Here!"

Terra ran through the camp. She tossed Lynai'seth's sword to her.

Lynai'seth caught it on the run. "What happened?"

"Oolo! Dav'yn convinced him it was safe to look for insects!"

"Terra, we're not meant for this. We need Jax and Marina!"

"Don't I know it. I was patching up Zwyna's bleeding foot."

They ran past G'unk-g'unks, past Outcasts, past the carts, over grass and rock. At one point, Lynai'seth jumped over a campfire, kicking a burst of sparks into the air.

They paused only once, to catch their breaths.

To hear Oolo scream.

They were on the trail again.

Lynai'seth hurried upstream. In a flash, she was at the rocky ledge. She leaned and jabbed her sword into the darkness.

Terra caught up with her. She was gasping for air. "Jax and Marina did this all the time."

"All the time," Lynai'seth repeated, still poking the air with her sword.

"And here I thought they were the lucky ones, getting out and travelling together."

Lynai'seth leaned under the rock. "I'll go first. It might be the white creature."

"No argument here."

Lynai'seth crawled under the ledge. She rolled onto the open ground, sprang to her feet and slashed the sword back and forth. "Oolo!" she called.

No answer.

Terra joined her. They started at the midpoint of the open area, then cautiously moved away from each other.

Lynai'seth stabbed open holes and empty air.

Terra took a step backward. Stopped.

Listened.

Turned sharply.

"Here!"

She knelt. In the light, she saw something.

A human hand.

She leaned more closely and studied it.

"NO —" Terra cried.

It was Oolo's hand. No body.

She wanted to turn away. Instead, she lifted the hand and packed it in her kit.

Lynai'seth was at her side. They crept forward. There had been signs of an attack and a struggle. Paw prints. Fur. Blood.

They found Oolo, on his back in a ditch.

Motionless.

"Let's get him out of there!" Terra said.

They reached down and carefully lifted his body which had been wedged in the ditch. His shirt had been shredded, his face, chest and arms had been clawed.

Terra leaned to listen to his heart.

"Is he —" Lynai'seth began.

"Let's go!"

They carried Oolo's limp body back to the ledge. They had to place him on the ground and slide him through the hollow. On the other side, they hurried downstream, back to camp. They placed him next to a campfire. Terra ran off, gathered her supplies and returned to Oolo's side.

The Outcasts huddled around Oolo. "What happened?" Gyro demanded.

"He was attacked," Lynai'seth said.

"By what? The white creature?"

"We didn't see."

"There!" Dav'yn cried. "THERE is your safe world!"

"Be quiet," Gyro warned.

"An innocent, attacked!"

"I said be quiet."

"Why — to silence the truth?"

Gyro swung an arm and batted Dav'yn to the ground. "I've had enough out of you!"

Dav'yn's mouth bled. Only Kg saw that instead of looking angered or hurt, Dav'yn smiled. "That's it," he said. "Fight with me instead of the real enemy."

S'yen knelt next to Terra. He handed her healing ointments made from the dead G'unk-g'unk. He helped her bandage Oolo's wounds.

Ru'an knelt by them. "His hand! It's gone!" she cried.

"*Hist,*" S'yen said, trying to silence her.

Lynai'seth tried moving the children away. "Back," she said. "Go back to your mats. Give Terra room to work."

The children began crying.

A girl screamed.

A boy got sick.

Some of the other Outcasts moaned, wailed, complained in their languages, uttered their fears. All the good will and gains of the day snapped like old bone.

"I know a way out of this," Dav'yn said, wiping blood from his face. "We don't have to be threatened every moment. And I won't hit you for disagreeing with me. Look at this poor, tortured boy. You could be next!"

For the first time, some of the Outcasts listened to him.

Dav'yn stood, wiped dust from his clothes and led four of the Outcasts to a dark part of the camp.

S'yen gently lifted Oolo's hand from Terra's open kit. He nodded to her.

"He thinks you can put it back on," Ru'an said.

"I've never done anything like this," Terra said. "I can't —"

"Try," Gyro said.

"I can't …"

"Try."

Terra looked up at Gyro and nodded. "Ru'an," she said, "please translate everything S'yen says as fast as you can."

"Okay. I will."

There was quick discussion among them about how to proceed. S'yen had been boiling a thick fluid in a nearby fire. The substance, drawn from the marrow of the dead G'unk-g'unk, would be used to seal Oolo's wrist, stop bleeding and fuse wrist bones to the hand.

Terra moved quickly. Her twelve fingers danced madly around Oolo's arm. She scraped his bones, peeling dead flesh away. She wiped blood that had caked on him. She began the impossible process of joining hand and wrist together again.

At one point, Terra screamed. "EEYAAHH!"

"What is it?" Gyro asked.

"I … can … feel his pain … in my own arm …"

"What?"

Lynai'seth knelt by them. "Terra says that healers in her community can feel the pain of their patients."

"Burning … " Terra said, wincing. "I … can't … move my hand …"

She stopped working on Oolo.

"Terra, please," Gyro said.

Tears streamed down her face. "I CAN'T!"

"For Oolo."

"He … may die anyway …"

"And he may live!"

"They never warned me … about the pain …"

"Who never warned you?"

"My people. My family. My mother."

"What would they do now?"

Terra shut her eyes. She breathed heavily.

Finally, she looked down at Oolo's hand.

She clenched her teeth.

And continued working.

Ru'an daubed medicines on Oolo's wounds. She cried while she worked. "Please, Oolo, please get well …"

S'yen helped Terra work her scalpel. She touched a nerve, and Oolo's arm twitched. Then he lay still as a shadow in the night. His heart didn't appear to be moving under his torn shirt.

It seemed to take Terra and S'yen forever to make any progress. Ru'an held a torch closely so that Terra could see the muscles, bones, veins and skin tissue.

"He's … lost so much blood …" Terra said.

Ru'an nodded. "We have G'unk-g'unk blood. He can drink it."

S'yen uttered an elaborate statement in his Avian tongue. Ru'an translated. "S'yen says once when he was a boy, he was showing off to friends and made a horrible mistake. He shot an arrow into a sacred bird. The bird fell to the ground. His friends ran away. His father found S'yen and the bird. The arrow had cut off a wing of the bird and was stuck to its body. *Hrr'kyen* — It is forbidden. His father took the bird home. He used medicines like we have here tonight."

"What happened?"

"The sacred bird died."

Terra smiled weakly. "That's — not encouraging."

"S'yen says he'll never let anything die in front of him again."

"He … can't control that. No one can."

"He won't give up. Neither will I."

Terra fought the pain tearing through her arm. "Count — me — in."

The twin moons arched across the night sky. The G'unk-g'unks shifted fitfully, perhaps aware of some threatening creature lurking in the darkness. Lynai'seth took the children to their mats. Other Outcasts kept their distance. One boy said he was afraid of Gyro. Another said he was afraid of everything.

Dav'yn and his four followers kept to themselves.

Gyro knelt by Terra. His skin was ashen gray. "I should not have hit Dav'yn," he said.

Terra shook her head. "If you hadn't, I would have."

"I failed his test."

"What test?"

"Of my patience."

"You've picked up the pieces and led us this far. That's saying a lot."

"The children will be afraid of me now. I acted the way an Antibody would."

"They — respect you. If they don't, we'll remind them of who you are."

Gyro rubbed her shoulders. "You're amazing. You're doing all this and still comforting me. Thank you."

"That's what healers are — AIEEEEE!"

"TERRA!"

She curled over Oolo's body, blind with pain. Her hand froze. It hung, useless, by her side.

"S'yen!" Gyro called.

S'yen nodded. He helped Terra continue weaving wrist and hand together, binding the bone, muscles and tissue. He dripped a thick balm over the entire wrist. Ru'an leaned with the torch. S'yen touched the torch to the balm. It burst into flames, shot sparks, then quickly died out.

Terra grabbed her aching, tortured wrist.

Oolo lay motionless.

His wrist smouldered. A foul-smelling smoke rose from his arm.

Silent moments passed.

Finally, Terra looked up. "It's over," she said.

Gyro held her. "Is he dead?"

"He's not quite dead yet," she said, "but he's not very alive, either."

In the distance, an animal howled at the two moons, its blood-curdling cry racing, rising, echoing and fading.

Its cry left the Outcasts shaking.

Chapter 18

"I need a cart, supplies and two of those bird creatures."

"No."

"I'm not asking — I'm telling you."

"I said 'no.'"

"You are in no position to argue with me, *Leader*," Dav'yn said to Gyro, his voice heavy with sarcasm.

The morning was raw and wet. A thick fog had fallen into the canyon and pressed like a gray blanket on them.

Dav'yn knelt by a small fire with his four new followers. He was stirring a pot of liquid.

Gyro's skin was as gray as the sky. "You five will stay here with us. It's dangerous to go off on your own."

"Dangerous to your leadership," Dav'yn said.

Gyro stood over him. "So this is why you stayed with the Outcasts? To tear us apart?"

"To keep you from killing yourselves. Tell me — exactly *where* is this HayVen you keep talking about?"

"Southwest."

"Exactly *where* southwest?"

"Quite a distance."

Dav'yn grinned. "You can't tell me. Or you don't know. Or you can't admit that HayVen is simply a fairy tale to keep these children fooled. I was left for lost in the desert. I've studied these lands. There are rocks, cliffs, foothills, then a plateau in the mountains to the southeast. It offers constant food, water, shelter and strategic safety. What can *you* offer?"

"Freedom."

"From what? What kind of freedom is there if you won't let the five of us go off on our own? You didn't seem to have a problem with my Master going off on her own with that Bubble-Headed Boy. She was quite pretty, you must admit."

"Be quiet."

"I will not!"

Dav'yn's voice scratched the air.

G'unk-g'unks opened wary eyes. Kg rolled on his side, awakening from a frightful dream about Antibodies.

He opened his eyes to an even more terrifying sight.

Dav'yn.

He saw what no one else did — Dav'yn sprinkling something from his pouch into the pot over the fire. Gyro had turned away to get more kindling for the fire and hadn't seen what Dav'yn was doing.

Kg had no control over his voice, his muscles, his bones, his body. He had been born with a disease that kept control of *him* in its own twisted manner. He was older than he looked — the same disease had stunted his growth.

Worker Antibodies had constructed hundreds of Food Cells around his community, poisoning the air, water and vegetation. Kg's mother and father had been forced to work in these Food Cells. They labored over hot, bubbling vats, creating murky compounds of unknown origin and destination. In the process, his parents had developed what Terra would term *lesions* on their organs. Kg was a product of these lesions. He was born diseased.

He could not open his mouth and cry out to anyone. He could not share the thoughts and impressions whirling in his mind. Sometimes he could not even lift his hand to his mouth to feed himself. Lynai'seth and the children always tried helping him, but none of them understood him. He was alive, screamingly alive, in the flesh-and-bone trap of his body.

All he could do was listen and watch.

"I'm preparing a warm drink," Dav'yn was telling Gyro. "We'll think more clearly with it. In my community it's called *morthea.*"

Gyro seemed interested in drinking the liquid.

Kg felt his heart racing and his spotted blue skin grow warm. He knew what was going to happen. He could not say or do anything about it.

The other children were still asleep. Kg tried rocking back and forth. His body lay still. It only jerked around when it wanted to, not when he wanted.

He could see Dav'yn slowly stirring the liquid, a secret smile curling across his face. Four boys sat cross-legged near him.

He has followers and they're going to poison Gyro, Kg realized.

Dav'yn nodded slightly. One of his followers slowly stood and wandered off in the fog in the direction of the carts.

Moments later, a second follower rose and headed in the direction of Yan.

Kg tried standing — no use. He tried working his arms and crawling. Failed again.

A part of him wanted to shut his eyes, go back to sleep, believe the terrible things he was seeing were simply part of a bad dream. Another part urged him to do something.

What?

He lay at least ten body lengths from them. There was little time to act.

He thought about Oolo, the only boy who had truly been kind to him. Oolo spoke to him in those funny rhymes and laughed as he ate bugs. Kg liked him. Kg had overheard that something had attacked Oolo, that he had lost his hand. He had overheard how Terra the healer bore up under tremendous pain to restore Oolo's hand.

If something bad happened to Gyro, then something bad would happen to Terra and Oolo and the kind Lynai'seth and the others.

Kg would not allow this.

Move. MOVE!

Something burned within him. Desire. He no longer thought of anything. He acted.

Kg was able to roll towards Dav'yn. Again. Again. He rolled face-down in the mud. He could smell the funk of wet earth. He could taste the grass. He stabbed his elbows in the mud, rocked his head and wiggled his shoulders.

And he moved.

Kg crept forward, little by little. He crept past sleeping Outcasts, past the G'unk-g'unks. Sweat from his forehead blinded him.

Then his body rebelled. His head twitched, his legs kicked. He lost what little control he had. As he rolled on his side, Kg saw Dav'yn raising a ladle from the liquid bubbling over the fire.

He heard Dav'yn say, "Give it a moment to cool."

Kg knew he had only one moment left.

He bit his lower lip. His eyes watered. He regained control over his body.

Five body lengths … four … three …

They hadn't seen him yet.

Two body lengths …

One of Dav'yn's followers was watching him. Dav'yn himself started to turn towards Kg.

Any moment now, they would stop him.

He had one chance, and only one chance.

He drew in a deep breath, hoisted himself up and kicked his leg forward. Kg's wild, twitching body flew into the fire. He knocked the pot off the wooden crossbar, splashing Dav'yn with the hot liquid.

Dav'yn screamed in pain. "YARRRR!" He threw the ladle in the air.

Kg's pants-leg caught on fire, but Gyro quickly patted it out.

Dav'yn squealed with pain. He locked his hands together over his head and swung his arms down to strike Kg's head like a hammer. "*MEPHISTE!*"

Gyro caught Dav'yn's hands in mid-air. And squeezed.

"YAGGH!" Dav'yn pulled himself backwards.

Dav'yn's two followers stood next to him, unsure of what to do.

Gyro rose. He seemed as tall as an ancient tree. His skin was crimson. "Get out! All of you! If this is how you are, you're of no use to us! Take a cart and go!"

The first of Dav'yn's followers had already stolen one of the carts and was whipping the two G'unk-g'unks harnessed to it. The second boy who had run in the direction of Yan approached with pieces of paper tucked under his arm. He had stolen Yan's writings about CH'NOPS for Dav'yn.

"I curse you and your Outcasts!" Dav'yn screamed. "Die out here! Let the animals feast on your rotting carcasses! If they don't stop you, I WILL!"

He hobbled away, holding his legs. The third and fourth boy followed.

The five of them got into the cart. Dav'yn stood and shook a fist. "You are Outcasts! We are SURVIVORS!" He snapped the reins, and the G'unk-g'unks reluctantly pulled away from camp, disappearing into the fog.

S'yen appeared pulling on his Battle Gloves.

Lynai'seth drew her sword.

Gyro raised his hand. "Let them go. We have to take care of Kg. He rolled all the way from his bed."

Kg felt the familiar spasms wrack his body. He sometimes felt he was nothing but a blanket being snapped in the air.

Gyro leaned over him. "We'll help you. It'll be all right."

Kg wanted to smile but couldn't. His head shook. Out of the corner of his eye, he saw some of Dav'yn's liquid on the ground. Kg didn't know if the poisonous plants that Dav'yn had used in the mixture were fatal to humans. He did see a lizard sneak from under a rock, drink some of the liquid, take a few unsure steps, stop and die.

No one would know that on this foggy day, Kg had fought in the hidden battleground of his body and had overcome the struggle with the spasms and pain.

No one would know that he had saved Gyro's life, and in doing so, had saved all of the Outcasts.

Chapter 19

The Outcasts walked in a fog through rocky terrain. No one spoke. The G'unk-g'unks moved at a steady pace. There was only the creaking of cart wheels, the moaning of wood, the clatter of pots and pans.

Each person seemed lost in thought. The vicious attack on Oolo had terrified everyone, despite Terra's miraculous healing of his hand. Dav'yn's departure from the group didn't surprise anyone — what surprised them was the four boys who joined Dav'yn. They had always been loyal to the group. Kon-gor, S'h'ta, Cobin-4 and Bayne were always among the first to agree with Gyro, the first to rise in the morning, the first to see hope in a world clouded with doubt.

Now they were gone.

Everything seemed to be fraying at the seams. The Outcasts, once strong as a group, seemed vulnerable and weak.

Some secretly blamed Gyro. They had seen him change from a bold leader defiant of Antibodies to a weak-willed *skrune* — a small, oily creature without a spine. They doubted his words that HayVen existed. They followed him simply because they couldn't think of anything else to do.

Gyro dropped back from the first cart to speak with Lynai'seth. His voice was low, his skin gray.

"Where were you this morning?" he asked.

"Scouting."

"Kg rolled free and almost burned himself."

"I know."

"You're not a scout. Jax and Marina are."

"They're not here."

Gyro paused. "So … what did you find while you were scouting?"

"Animal tracks."

"What kind?"

"I thought it might have been that white creature I've been seeing." Lynai'seth paused. "But I believe they were Shadow Beasts."

"How many?"

"Four."

Gyro wiped his face. "I thought the Shadow Beasts were our allies. They helped us fight Antibodies. Why would they attack Oolo?"

"It looks as if it was a mother with her three babies. I think Oolo got between them. That's always dangerous."

"*Baby* Shadow Beasts?"

"There were tiny sets of five prints around what looked like a nest."

Gyro looked past Lynai'seth at the trail behind them. His skin tone subtly shifted, turning a shade of purple. "They're multiplying."

"That could be good."

"Let's hope."

"*Hope.* You use that word often. Do you really believe it?" Lynai'seth asked.

Gyro stroked this thin beard thoughtfully. "When everything fails, it's all that's left. My family believed in HayVen. I can do no less."

"You lost Dav'yn and the four others."

"They'll be back."

"Maybe. Will you forgive them?"

"There's nothing to forgive," Gyro said. "They haven't done me any harm."

"They've made some of the group doubt you."

Gyro smiled. "I often doubt myself. I never wanted to be a leader. I was betrothed to be married in five Sun Cycles. We were going to open a school for orphans."

"What was she like — the one you were to marry?"

"Her name was Calyssta Saine Ty," Gyro said. "She lived in a *b'kki* – a country village in our community. I saw her the first time while she was teaching children in the shade of a tree. She used to say, 'Where there is a tree, there is a school.' She always smiled and sang and teased me. She believed all things were precious and important."

Gyro and Lynai'seth paused a moment to honor her memory.

"She is the reason I formed the Outcasts," Gyro admitted. "It seems like ages ago. The Antibodies attacked our community. The battle was worse than anything I could have imagined — terrible and swift. I was beaten senseless, left for dead. When I recovered, my village was cold and silent. My family was gone. I ran to the *b'kki* and found Calyssta Saine Ty near her favorite tree. She was dying. She whispered one word: 'HayVen.' Then she died in my arms."

Lynai'seth watched as Gyro's skin tones changed from deep purple to a chalky white shade, the color of mourning and grief. He had said once that his skin colors reflected his emotions, but there was no way of telling exactly what his emotions were. He seemed angry, then quiet, then reflective.

"So I've decided to save anyone I can," Gyro continued. "It will never make up for the loss of my community and Calyssta, but it's all I can do to give my life any meaning."

Gyro turned away and walked towards the rattling row of carts. Lynai'seth watched as he adjusted a blanket for Oolo who was motionless and silent, more a corpse than a boy. He asked Zwyna about her injured foot. He teased some of the children. He patted the G'unk-g'unks. He spoke with the leaders of each of the carts. As he took control of the group once again, his skin tone changed to a healthy brown color.

Lynai'seth returned to her children. She understood her duties better. She would leave the scouting to others and serve Gyro's band of orphans as best she could, until her final breath.

***

A new world unfolded before them. During their adventures, the Outcasts had crossed open fields, stark, unforgiving deserts, cracked land and imposing mounds of rock. They had descended into the crystal caves and sparkling underground river, hoping they were the "angles of rainbows" that Yan had seen in a dream long ago. The Outcasts had risen to a plateau, had watched in horror as the planet trembled and rocks fell, forever sealing Marina and Jax in the maze of caves.

They had travelled in the G'unk-g'unk carts through valleys where rocky walls rose in a wavering array of colors from yellow to deep blue.

Now, while the G'unk-g'unks moved at a brisk pace, they dipped into a canyon that turned a magnificent golden hue — the fog lifted, the clouds parted and the sun stroked its length and breadth like a loving hand. The path was wide and flat. It dipped at an angle so slight that no one noticed.

Children dozed in the warm light. The leaders of the carts let their reins slip, and the G'unk-g'unks took control of the direction and distance they would travel.

Gyro shifted, as if something had caught his attention. Then he eased into his place on the lead cart.

He held up his hand. His arm had turned golden, like the light pouring into the canyon. He looked back at the Outcasts. The others had turned to gold. Even the G'unk-g'unks and the carts they pulled seemed cast in amber light.

Lynai'seth drew back her sleeve a bit and looked at her arm. Her skin was a warm, light purple color, like the lilacs that had once adorned her Shi'vaal Community before the Antibodies had struck. Now, in canyon light, she too had turned to gold.

During another time of higher spirits, the children might have jumped from their carts and danced in the light. Now, they hesitated. Despite the warm promise of this canyon light, they had grown afraid of everything. Their spirits seemed as lifeless as Oolo.

One of the Outcasts muttered about how Kon-gor, S'h'ta, Cobin-4 and Bayne would have enjoyed the strange light, how they had disappeared right under Gyro's nose. How Gyro had let them go away. How they might be lost to the final darkness …

Gyro walked from cart to cart, trying to rouse everyone's spirits, trying to get them to enjoy the play of light, but the most he could evoke was a weak smile from Mohir'a'qest. He was more concerned with Zwyna's injured foot. She was in no mood to compete with him on anything, and he felt lost without her spirit.

Little Klanga held Feelie up before her. The pumpkin animal looked like a ball of pure gold. Feelie purred, pleased with the sensation of light on its fur.

Lynai'seth watched. Only Feelie had given this day — and Gyro — the proper respect. She gently roused the children from their naps. "Look," she said softly. "We're all the same color."

The ever-cheerful Alamine giggled. His twin, Amina, smiled.

Lynai'seth sang, her melody as golden as the sky. Some of the children lifted their heads like morning flowers to light.

Gyro paused to enjoy the song. He shut his eyes and listened.

He allowed himself only a moment of peace. Something again caught his attention.

Terra stepped next to him. "What is it?"

Gyro paused. He sniffed the air. "Smoke."

"I don't see any smoke."

"It's out there."

"Where?"

"Ahead."

Terra looked into the distance. "I don't see anything."

"I can smell it," Gyro said. "It's an — ability — that I have. My mother said that ever since I was young I've had a nose for trouble. My father said I could track a scent better than a hunting dog."

Terra grinned. "Okay, puppy — what kind of smoke is it?"

Gyro closed his eyes and breathed deeply. "Friendly. But mixed with a warning."

"What does that mean?"

Gyro watched the carts. "I'm not sure. The G'unk-g'unks don't seem worried, and they're far more advanced than we are. Let's follow their lead and move with extreme caution."

He ran off to the lead cart and jumped up onto the seat with surprising agility for someone his size. Gyro seized the reins, then snapped them. The G'unk-g'unks responded by speeding up the pace.

The golden light deepened to amber, as if the sky and surrounding rock had been dipped in honey. All the Outcasts sat up in attention. Nothing had happened, but there was an air of expectation, as if something important *were* about to occur at any moment.

The Outcasts were silent, but the G'unk-g'unks began talking to each other. The lead animal pulling Gyro's cart spoke in loud, commanding tones, and it did indeed sound as if it were repeatedly calling out, "*Gunk, gunk!*" in a deep, throaty voice. It made the sound three times. The birds pulling the second cart replied, then added a fourth call of "*gunk, gunk.*" The sounds rolled from the depths of their long throats and seemed to burst in the air, bounce off the rocks and fade into space. There were long calls punctuated with short cries of "*gunk — gunk, gunk!*"

An elaborate bird language swirled through the canyon. It didn't interrupt the world as much as it became a part of it, a natural expression of wind, plant, rock and animal existing in harmony. The Outcasts seemed to be the only ones out of place in this vast stretch of creation.

There was no urgency to the conversation, no increasing frequency or volume. These were not distress calls but warning signals. The feathered creatures fanned out into a V-formation, like migrating birds. It was a highly efficient formation. The strongest birds were up front to withstand the worst of any surprise attacks. The swiftest birds were at the farthest points of the V-formation. They would be able to dash past predators and surround them. The V-formation would turn into an encircling O.

Lynai'seth walked next to Ru'an. "It's amazing we were able to tame any of these animals at all."

"We didn't tame them," Ru'an said. "They tamed us."

Her comment made sense. Once the Outcasts felt they had conquered the G'unk-g'unks, they stopped attacking them.

These were clever birds.

Their footfalls seemed lighter, as if they were sneaking up on enemies.

The older Outcasts instinctively reached for weapons in the carts: swords, spears, bow and arrows. The children took up slingshots and rocks.

The path narrowed. The G'unk-g'unks tightened their V-formation. They curved downhill. They moved under an arching bridge of turquoise rock, as if entering the portal of an unknown, ancient kingdom.

Walls of rock rose to either side of them. The formations looked like long, giant faces peering with disgust down at them.

Gyro pulled back on his reins, bringing his cart to a halt. He squinted at a wall of rock, so close he could have leaned and touched it.

"Petroglyphs," he muttered.

At first, the markings on the amber wall of rock seemed invisible. On closer inspection, though, tiny scratches and markings appeared in the creamy yellow light. Gyro saw semi-circles, circles, crescent shapes, diamonds, scimitar curves, dots, slashes and lettering that bore combinations of these shapes. The arches imitated the rocky portal under which they had just passed.

S'yen dropped from a cart, slipped off a Battle Glove, and carefully ran his hand along the slick, shiny rock until it came to rest on a most fantastic image.

Someone had carved a majestic figure of a G'unk-g'unk, forever sealed in a transparent glaze on the rocky wall.

S'yen lowered his head. Ru'an stepped next to him, looked at the image and also lowered her head in homage. Together they spoke what might have been a poem of respect in their elaborate Avian language.

Terra looked at Xalid, but he was unable to keep up with what they were saying. "I think the image has religious importance to them," he guessed. "I believe they're praying."

"They think these birds are deities?"

"Not exactly. More like helpers working on behalf of a greater plan."

"No argument here."

Terra heard Oolo moan. She turned to him. The hand she had achingly repaired lifted as if under its own will, like a young bird first taking flight. Oolo looked as if he were answering a teacher's question. The hand dipped and rose in slow, even waves.

Klanga gasped with astonishment at the sight. The other children watched, and something deep in them stirred. Something elusive and easily lost, something that died as quickly as troubles began.

It was Gyro's favorite word.

Hope.

The children did not rise in a sudden laugh or cry of joy — they slowly began to realize there was something rich and wonderful beyond their own dim trials. They watched Oolo's hand as one might study the fluttering of a butterfly.

The dance of Oolo's hand in the brown-golden air made them realize *anything was possible.*

The G'unk-g'unks proceeded slowly past the wall etchings. The pictures became more detailed and elaborate, telling an entire history in this grand museum of rock. There were more G'unk-g'unks depicted on the rock, golden birds with feathers spread like a queen's fan. A series of petroglyphs showed insects crawling along the ground, creeping through a mist or watery substance, then growing and walking on their two hind legs like humans.

In a battle scene that covered a large portion of the rock wall, warriors with snouts, fangs, thick manes and sharp claws fought these upright insects. Birds with three eyes swooped from a gleaming sky to drop weapons for the insects behind the battle lines. Widespread fires raged. In the distance, dark clouds rolled ominously.

Then there was a blank space along the wall.

Then, a scene of sunrise: a simple curve of horizon and a semi-circle of morning sun lifting its eager eye.

Oolo's hand still danced in the air.

Terra glanced for a moment to see something even more amazing than the battle scene on the wall. Kg sat up. He was not struggling with his bones and muscles. He simply sat up as a normal child would on a cool, calm morning after a long night of sleep.

"Kg?" Lynai'seth said.

"Hi," he said with a smile.

Terra squinted in puzzlement. "What's going on here?"

The Outcasts turned away from the pictures on the wall and gathered around Oolo and Kg.

Zwyna clapped her hands with joy. "Look!" she said. "The cut in my foot went away!"

Mohir'a'qest beamed. Zwyna was his main competition in life, but he had felt completely lost without her.

Terra looked around at the group. "How do you feel?" she asked everyone.

They had had cuts, bruises, fractured bones, sore muscles, pounding headaches. They had felt hungry, tired and terrified for so long.

The Outcasts spoke in their native tongues.

"They feel good," Xalid said, translating as many languages as he could. "No aches, no pains."

"Everyone?"

"Everyone. How do you feel?"

Terra thought for a moment. "The best in a long time."

Gyro joined them. Some of the Outcasts applauded, nodded, smiled, patted his back, gestured their approval and praise.

Finally, little Klanga put their feelings to words in the Common Tongue. "You brought us to HayVen!"

"HayVen!" the children chanted.

"HayVen! HayVen!"

Lynai'seth stepped forward. "I don't feel tired anymore. Is this —"

"I don't know," Gyro said. "We need to be cautious."

"Gyro! Gyro!" children cried.

"Wait!" he said. "Let's keep exploring!"

Too late. The children jumped from their carts and ran in sweeping circles. The G'unk-g'unks seemed amused, tapping a beat with their large webbed feet.

"We passed through golden light," Terra said. "We're all healed. This *must* be HayVen. We may be able to find our families. You did it!"

"I didn't do anything," Gyro said.

"You gave us hope when there wasn't any."

"You gave Oolo hope when there wasn't any," he said.

"You promised us HayVen, and here it is!"

"I'm not sure yet, Terra."

"We lost our homes. Our loved ones. We lost Jax and Marina. We've all suffered. There are no Antibodies here, as far as I can see. We're all getting stronger. What do you make of Oolo's hand if this isn't HayVen? What about Kg?"

"It's like any new experiment," Gyro said. "We have to study it further."

"Well," Terra said, "I'm studying it with the children!" She hurried to Oolo's side.

Xalid produced a small flute. He played a tune of celebration. Mohir'a'qest handed Zwyna a drum, and she pounded it with glee.

"Something isn't right," Gyro told Lynai'seth. "If this were HayVen, Marina and Jax would be here to greet us. Our families would rush to us. Ancestors would hold us close and kiss our foreheads."

"Maybe that's around the corner," Lynai'seth said with a faint smile. She unfastened her sword and returned it to her cart.

For the first time in their long journey together, the Outcasts celebrated. They felt young energy filling their bodies and lifting their hearts. They didn't talk about hope and joy — they *became* hope and joy.

They sang and danced and laughed.

They didn't notice something moving along the ground through the amber light.

They didn't hear the warning cries of the G'unk-g'unks.

They didn't see that there were two creatures approaching.

The creatures were four-legged. Huge.

White, even in the engulfing amber light.

Their fur and flesh were transparent so that anyone with the nerve to look could see their bones, muscles, eyeballs and beating hearts.

They weren't Antibodies. They weren't Shadow Beasts.

Lynai'seth recognized one of the creatures. It was the white beast that had been following them. With a partner.

Everyone froze as the creatures lifted their throats, bared their teeth and shrieked with unholy abandon, their cries filling the amber canyon with new white fear.

Chapter 20

Somewhere beyond caves, cliffs and canyons, beyond the crystal rainbows underground and the layers of red, green and blue rock aboveground, beyond lands nourished with glistening waters and washed in golden light, beyond all things experienced or even imagined, something watched.

Separate from the world of sweet skies, curving land, one sun and twin moons, something broke from its vast, patterned movement, buckled and stopped.

Had a human done this, it might have been considered anger, even rage.

This broken movement was greater than rage, a higher and unspeakably deeper level.

In the mist that now surrounded all things, bright green, yellow and red lights swirled as they had for ages. Lances of pure white light shot through the fog-like needles in the unimaginable pattern of an enormous, world-spanning tapestry.

Diamonds appeared in what might have been called the sky, if there had been any way to determine what was up or down. The diamonds pulsed, not by reflecting light from an outside source, but from the light within them.

Beneath, behind and above the diamonds, glowing golden strings vibrated.

The ground, if it could be called that, slithered about, with squares, circles, triangles, rectangles, zigzags and crescent shapes falling, sliding, erupting and organizing.

The ground organized itself into a magnificent pattern that began with a few simple shapes and repeated from a center point, outward, to create an even more profound pattern that might have only been fully seen from the remote vantage point of one of Dulunae's moons.

If such a thing were possible, the shapes were becoming a living language, bursting with creative life and individuality, then settling into an organization through which intelligent beings could understand each other. The shapes did not read left to right or right to left, top to bottom or bottom to top. The shapes did not read at diagonals. This was a language that lifted from the two dimensions of length and width to five, ten, thousands of dimensions higher, where shapes looped back into themselves in eternal figure-eight patterns, danced with human notions of time such as past, present and future and glided to a place and time where answers occurred even before questions were asked.

If a single word could be used to describe this realm, this entity, it would be one that few even knew. Those who did know were afraid to utter it. Those who did utter it, died in a blinding flash of light.

The mindless ones were allowed to use the vague term "INITIATING ELEMENTAL." Those on Dulunae — burdened with small, human fears — built shrines to it, as if statues, monuments, temples, buildings carved of stone and ivory and adorned with jewels could in any way pay homage to this "INITIATING ELEMENTAL" and thus ease their fears.

A few who spoke the word were allowed to live, the reason

for their lives being spared as fogged and mysterious as this realm with no up or down.

The word no one dared speak was CH'NOPS.

Pitiful little Outcast creatures that should not have survived were making their way with the Ancient Birds to the Amber Chambers. They had passed through golden light and had healed their wounds and injuries.

Unacceptable ...

Unpardonable ...

They should never have discovered that the easing of pain was possible in their short lifetimes.

The Alignment of the Twin Moons was fast approaching, when the Dulunae that all creatures knew would cease to exist.

CH'NOPS was not about to let anything — or anyone — interfere.

It was time to make its presence known.

Swiftly.

Clearly.

Brutally.

Chapter 21

The planet Dulunae had endured countless Sun Cycles. A brutal collision of stars had brought this massive planet to life ages ago, before the clocks of time had begun their repetitive measuring of moments. No clocks had existed at Dulunae's birth; it had been a violent birth in the boundless black void and deep heavens, full of expanding gases, spiralling flames and molten, whirling earth.

The brightest star, the sun, had plucked five lifeless mounds of rock like a child lifting pebbles from a stream and had tugged them into its orbit. The largest became Dulunae. Two of the smaller starborn rocks became Dulunae's twin moons.

After innumerable Sun Cycles, chain reactions at the smallest levels occurred, and Dulunae was born. Suddenly, after aeons, there was water. Where there was water, there was life. Trees grew, providing shade for plants and tall grasses. Their seeds drifted on the wind, sprinkling distant lands with verdant hope. Eventually animals feasted on the vegetation.

To those marking time, Dulunae was ancient, existing beyond the limits of human imagination. In a greater scheme, it was an infant, full of vitality unprecedented in all the cosmos.

Dulunae had known its share of conflicts between old and new. Entire continents shifted and resettled in new configurations on the face of the planet. This, in turn, affected the flow of water, the climate, the types of plants and animals that survived.

When human communities dotted the planet, another type of conflict arose, the endless mortal combats of humans — forever trying to enslave other people in the name of new world orders.

The outcomes were all the same. Generations died. The dust of Dulunae won.

In this most recent Sun Cycle, a new game was being played, so profound that it pulled CH'NOPS with the force of gravity into a most human set of situations on Dulunae.

On this Planet of Two Moons, a tiny group of Outcasts stood petrified with fear in the Amber Chambers, where vicious white beasts threatened them.

Elsewhere, in a place the Outcasts had left behind, deep in the earth under mounds of fallen rock, something stirred.

A single pebble bounced down a pile of rock, dirt and dust.

A second pebble fell. A third.

Something was struggling to find air.

Silence. Stillness.

Then —

— a hand.

A valiant hand poked from the rock and rubble like a plant. It quivered, much the way Oolo's hand had fluttered before the wall paintings on the amber rock.

Then it stopped.

It was scarred, scratched, bruised and bleeding. It looked like the dread marking of a freshly dug tomb.

No great history on this tombstone, no epic poem for the ages. Only the unknown struggle of someone who refused to quit.

The ground screamed. "EEEEYAAAHHH!"

Two hands grabbed, clawed, dug. Gradually, a head appeared from its burial place.

"AAAHHH!"

It looked like a strange melon, coated with damp black fur, adorned with pointed protrusions.

Marina.

Alive and struggling.

She coughed, choked, spat and frantically wiped mud, clay, dust and dirt from her face.

She fought with fallen earth.

And won.

Marina paused to catch her breath. There was an eerie silence in the cave chamber.

No Shadow Beasts, no crimson Octinids, no oozing creatures with their hideous multiple eyes.

Nothing.

She listened. She strained her ears to hear something.

Yes —

Tap, tap, tap.

The same sound she had heard before diving into the passage to escape the crimson Octinids.

As she struggled, part of the wall gave way, revealing a dull patch of mossy green light. Water dripped from an unknown source.

Strange, yellow subterranean plants were growing blindly in the dim light.

Food!

Marina scrambled to reach the plants. She plucked a handful. The plants had long, stringy leaves and thick purple stems. At the top of each stem grew what looked like bright yellow onion bulbs. They didn't look like anything poisonous that Yan had found on their travels.

Her parents had experimented with growing vegetables underwater — not in the salt water of the sea but a more refined, purified water. She remembered eating tomatoes the size of her fist.

Marina snapped off a bulb, stripped it clean and sniffed it. The bulb had a sweet fragrance and rich juices that made her stomach tighten. She took a careful bite, chewed, swallowed. Bit again. Again.

"Whoa!" she jerked backwards. The digested bulb coursed through her bloodstream, immediately reviving her from head to foot. She ate a second bulb. A third.

She jumped to her feet. She was battered and bruised but somehow felt alive again, full of an energy she hadn't known since her days at home in the Quae Community.

She gathered the bulbs. Some were bright red, others yellow, purple or deep blue. In a distant corner of the chamber, she found bulbs that were bright orange.

Marina harvested the bulbs, drank from the pools of water in which these fantastic plants grew.

Her hearing grew sharp as a steel blade. The tapping noise seemed to be pounding nearby. Marina looked into the dim gray light and easily spotted a passageway in the direction of the tapping. She followed it.

She was by the underground river again. The fight between Shadow Beasts and oozing creatures had long since ended and had gone its route to other dark regions. She looked left and right but saw no Octinids or other threatening creatures.

She heard only the repeated tapping.

There was a rhythm to the noise like —

— *a signal!*

Marina ran along the river. The tapping sounded like a heartbeat, regular and vital. She reached three chambers. The tapping came from the chamber on her left. No hesitation this time.

She followed a curve, gliding her hands along the slick, wet walls.

She paused to listen.

The tapping stopped as sudden and sure as death.

Marina hurried through the passage. She climbed through a narrow opening, worked her way down a dark corridor, turned a corner and slammed to a halt.

There was a crumpled form on the ground.

In its hand, her quarterstaff.

"JAX!"

Marina lunged to the side of her fallen companion. She turned him onto his back.

"JAX!"

Marina cried tears of joy. She hugged him, then placed him back on the ground.

She leaned closely, listening for his breath. Felt his wrist for a pulse, as Terra had shown her.

"No … not now … I won't let you die …"

She didn't know the *resuscitation* technique Terra had taught Jax, finding it too repulsive at the time. Instead, she crossed her hands and repeatedly pressed down on his chest. She had seen Terra revive a child's heart in this way. The pressure had to be precise, rhythmic.

The small moments seemed eternal. Finally, Jax jumped, then settled.

His eyes opened in thin slits.

"Jax, it's Marina. We're alive."

"Muh …" he muttered, trying to say her name.

"Rest. I have food."

Marina pulled an orange bulb from her pocket. She placed it by his mouth, but he was too weak to chew. Marina bit the bulb and chewed it into a paste. She mixed the paste with a trickle of juice and water and slipped the concoction into his mouth.

Jax choked. Gagged. But finally swallowed.

Took small bites of the orange bulb.

And slowly revived, the bulb racing though his bloodstream to work its wonders on him.

"Marina," he said, smiling weakly up at her.

"I'm here."

"Marina."

"Here, Jax. Don't talk. Eat."

Jax reached for the quarterstaff and tried lifting it to her. "I found this … thought it was someone's bones … I saved it for you …"

"I know, Jax."

"Tapped … our signals … to give you a way out …"

"I know." Marina sat against the rock wall and pulled Jax onto her lap. She peeled the wet cloak from his face. His face looked mangled, his eyes swollen and battered.

"Marina, I —"

"Shhh. Sleep."

"I —"

"Shh."

Jax closed his eyes. "I see —"

"Yes, you'll be able to see."

" … see that I love …"

Jax fell asleep.

Marina cradled him.

And secretly wished he had finished saying the name of the person he loved.

Chapter 22

They rested in the stillness of the caves.

Jax finally awoke. "Oh!"

Marina looked down at him. "What's wrong?"

"Am I dreaming?"

"I don't think so."

"Marina, I wake up, and the first person I see is *you*. This must be a dream." Jax climbed to his knees and hugged her. "Dream or not, thank you for saving me."

"No thanks are necessary. You did well on your own."

This time, Marina didn't hit him in the face. She hugged him back.

They lingered.

Marina reluctantly leaned away from him. She stood and took up her quarterstaff. "We have to get out of here," she said. "The caves are crawling with monsters."

"The last things I heard were Shadow Beasts and those creatures from the river."

"At one point, I was covered in red Octinids and thick webs. I almost choked to death."

Jax gasped. "We have to get out of here."

Marina leaned on her quarterstaff and helped him stand. Jax was still woozy. Marina quickly slid a helpful arm around him and guided him through the cave.

"Your quarterstaff is amazing," Jax said. "I didn't use it to find a way to safety. It seemed to find the way for me."

"And I heard it tapping," Marina said. "So the staff brought us together again. For good."

Jax turned to her and smiled. "You think?"

"I know."

They walked for a while through the dim subterranean world. The light had shifted. The crystal walls no longer sparkled. They looked like dull and dusty mirrors lost in storage.

Jax leaned away from Marina for a moment. He widened his eyes and stared into the heavy gloom. "I don't know what's in those plants you fed me," he said, "but my eyesight is perfect again."

"I gave you the orange ones. I hoped they had … what do you call it?"

"*Kyrota,*" Jax said. "I think they did. How do *you* feel?"

"Better than ever."

"Are there any more plants?"

"I harvested all of them," Marina said. "They should keep us alive, for a time."

Jax stared. "I see something."

"Where?"

"About fifty paces to the right. On that small ledge."

They hurried to the spot. Marina lifted a small piece of cloth.

"I know what that is," Jax said excitedly. "It's one of Lynai'seth's hair ribbons."

The mention of her name soured Marina's mood. "How do you know?"

"Look. It has the markings of her community on it. It's a sign."

"Sign of what? Sloppiness?"

"She would never leave one of these behind. It's a clue to

where they went. We just have to figure it out." Jax studied the cloth. "Lynai'seth said that she wore three ribbons on each side. Two represented her family, the other four represented directions and landscapes. Look at the way this is twisted. It's not her family. She wouldn't bind their names in a knot. It's a direction."

"How do you know?" Marina wondered. "She's never spoken to you."

"Not directly," Jax admitted, "but she told the children, and Klanga explained everything to me."

"I'm sure she did."

Jax turned to Marina. "Didn't Lynai'seth tell *you* about her language?"

Marina poked the ground with her quarterstaff. "I must have missed that lesson. Too busy scouting for safe camp."

"Safe camp. That's where they are. We just have to learn how to follow them."

Marina noticed pieces of Lynai'seth's hair on the ribbon, thin and lustrous as golden thread. Marina's hair felt like rope.

"Is this north or south?" Jax wondered. "East or west?"

"Not much of a clue if we can't figure it out."

"I have to think about what Klanga said about Lynai'seth's culture."

"Don't spend too much time on that," Marina said. "We have to find a way out of here. Let's keep going."

"Wait. The letters look like small pictures. Drawings. It's a language based on art. If I remember, it reads right to left, then curves down, left to right, then up to the right corner again. The simple part, that is."

"I think I hear Shadow Beasts."

"These shapes look like ice. And this part of the ribbon is white. That could mean the polar caps. Meaning north or south."

"We need to move!"

"But the ribbon is twisted to the right a little. That could mean northeast."

"Jax," Marina said, "northeast is vast and wide."

Jax turned to her and smiled. "You called me by my name. You've never called me by my name."

"Yes, I have — thousands of times."

"Not like the way you just said it. Warmly."

"Is there something wrong with using someone's name?"

"Not a thing. *Marina.*"

Her skin suddenly tingled. "What — what else did you find in the ribbon? Any other clues?"

"No. You're right. Northeast is vast. They could be anywhere."

"Don't give up yet," Marina urged. "You say she would never leave a hair tie behind. She left it on a small ledge here. Maybe that has a purpose, too."

"You're right! Didn't you and I see those plateaus northeast of here before entering the caves?"

"Yes. It's worth a try. First we have to find a way out of here."

Marina offered an arm, but Jax was strong enough to walk on his own. They followed the same route that they had used to enter the caves with the Outcasts. They easily approached the cave entrance but found piles of crumbled rock and boulders blocking the passageway.

"It would take us forever to dig through all that," Jax said.

"Let's keep looking," Marina said. "Use those special eyes of yours."

Jax nodded. "I will."

He climbed over a pile of rocks, crawled on his stomach and reached a pocket of air and light. "Marina!"

"I'm on it."

They crawled into the pocket. There was a boulder jammed in the passageway, but radiant sunlight poured through the many openings between rock and cave wall.

Marina ran her hands along the boulder. "We can wedge my staff into this opening and pry open an exit."

"We might break your quarterstaff."

"It's stronger than you think."

"But it's everything to you, Marina. It's all you have."

"What are the alternatives?"

"Keep looking for another way out."

"That could take a long time. We don't have a long time. I heard something down the river." Marina jammed the quarterstaff into an opening near the base of the boulder, rubbed her hands together and grabbed the staff. Her arm muscles tightened. She looked over her shoulder at Jax. "Are you with me?"

Jax smiled. "Always." He stepped next to Marina and grabbed the staff.

"On three: one, two, three!"

"YARRGHH!" they both shouted.

Marina and Jax pulled on the quarterstaff. It bent. The

boulder didn't budge.

They struggled.

Nothing.

"Let go!" Marina said.

They relaxed their grip. The staff snapped back and forth, then fell to the ground.

Rather than place the quarterstaff in an open space, Marina loosely held the staff and let it drop from her hand, as if the *staff* were choosing the best place to form a wedge.

"Again," Marina said. "One, two, three!"

They tugged the quarterstaff. Gritted their teeth and pulled. The staff bent, curving into the shape of a bow.

Marina winced. Jax also shut his eyes.

The quarterstaff groaned, as if about to snap in half.

Marina's ears twitched. There was a familiar growling somewhere behind them. "Shadow Beasts! PULL!"

They redoubled their efforts. Their hands burned. Muscles ached.

The boulder sat.

The first crimson Octinid dropped onto Jax's shoulder.

No passageway, no tunnel, no escape this time.

The growling grew louder. Octinids coiled their web around Marina's legs.

"You were … right … about the Octinids … " Jax said through his teeth.

A splinter popped from the quarterstaff.

Growling echoed in the cave chamber.

Octinid webbing tightened like rope around Marina's ankles. Six Octinids dropped from the ceiling, through shafts of sunlight, onto Jax's hood. One crawled towards his eyes.

The boulder sat.

The quarterstaff seemed to be humming, ringing, screeching for mercy.

Red Shadow Beast eyes dotted the passage behind them.

No escape.

Marina and Jax made a final effort.

The quarterstaff also made its final effort.

The boulder — the massive, motionless chunk of rock — budged.

Shifted.

Moved.

Sunlight poured over them.

When the rock moved, part of the cave wall disintegrated and collapsed, giving them enough space to crawl outside.

"COME ON!" Marina grabbed the quarterstaff, scrambled through the opening, extended a hand and pulled Jax.

They rolled outside, into the sunlight, downhill, onto the ground. A Shadow Beast furiously clawed at the small passage, digging its way after them.

"I thought the Shadow Beasts were our friends!" Jax said. He turned to the creature madly clawing through the opening. "I thought you were our friends!"

The Shadow Beast pushed its head through the opening.

Marina jumped to her feet and grabbed his arm. "We can discuss this later!"

She pulled him towards the northeastern plateaus.

A dark cloud filled the sky.

While Marina and Jax ran, thousands of black birds shot

through the bright sky in the opposite direction. Larger, green-feathered birds followed. Enormous, rainbow-colored snakes writhed, twisted, slid over each other by the thousands. Vile birds with long, snapping beaks devoured some of the snakes, then continued their flight south.

None of the fleeing creatures gave Jax or Marina any notice. If the creatures had been able to speak in a common voice, they might have cried one word: *survival.*

"Something is terrifying these animals," Marina said.

Jax jumped over snakes. "Something is terrifying *me.*"

"Still want to climb the plateaus?"

"Maybe. Any clues from your quarterstaff?"

Marina held it over her head. "It's not resisting us."

"That's not much to go on."

"We have to find the rest of the Outcasts. If you believe the hair ribbon is a clue, let's follow it."

Brown clouds loomed, not in the sky, but ahead of them. There was a rumbling and thunderous echo.

Whatever was scaring the animals was heading right towards them.

Chapter 23

Shadow Beasts.

Hundreds of them.

Or thousands.

Charging at Marina and Jax with the force of a typhoon, their dust a towering brown pillar that swept from the ground and darkened the sky.

Their snarling was deafening.

Jax and Marina could not hear a word from each other.

There was no time to discuss.

No time to think.

Only act.

Jax spotted a ledge in the direction of the Shadow Beasts. He pointed to it. Marina nodded, ran and vaulted up onto it with her quarterstaff. She held out a hand. Jax ran and jumped, barely grabbing Marina. She pulled him up onto the ledge. They scrambled up the side of a plateau, using pockets of rock as handholds. They climbed the sheer face of the slick rock, higher and higher. Marina led, relying on her natural instincts to scale the plateau. Jax followed her every move.

They were both clinging to the side of the plateau as the storm of Shadow Beasts swept below them.

"HOLD ON!" Marina shouted, but Jax couldn't hear her.

They shut their eyes. Pebbles and rocks showered down on them, dust blew furiously. The force of wind threatened to tear them from the wall.

Shadow Beasts fought with each other, snapped their jaws and swung claws in the air. One of them jumped, swung an arm at Jax's leg, missed and fell on top of other Shadow Beasts.

All forms of animal life raced ahead of the Shadow Beasts. Many of the birds survived. Many of the snakes did not. The G'unk-g'unks had known well in advance that the Shadow Beasts would attack and had been able to carry away the Outcasts.

Marina and Jax clung to the rock wall. The dust storm whirled around them and seemed as if it would never end. Dust pellets struck their skin.

Another Shadow Beast jumped in the air. Marina heard its fierce cry and tugged Jax to safety just as the Shadow Beast struck. Its claws scratched sparks along the rock.

"LET'S GO!" Marina pulled Jax's arm. He squinted, watching her move up the wall. They grappled with the fury of the wind.

Higher, higher …

Jax's foot slipped. He quickly regained his balance.

Finally, Marina worked her way over the top of the plateau. She helped Jax. They crawled with their elbows until they could lie flat on the top.

They then turned and peeked down over the edge. The Shadow Beasts continued to charge through the passage below them.

"This can't be good," Jax said. "Where are they going? What are they doing?"

"You could go down and ask them."

Jax looked at her. "You're making fun of me. I can tell."

Marina looked at his hood. Part of it was wiggling. She reached over and pulled it off his round pink head.

"Hey!"

"Jax, there's an Octinid on your head."

"Very funny." Jax reached up and touched the creature. "AH! There's an Octinid on my head!"

He quickly threw it over the edge. In one deft move, a Shadow Beast leapt through the air, devoured the Octinid and kept running.

Marina and Jax watched in horror — and awe — as the Shadow Beasts kept storming through the passage. It seemed as if a volcano of Shadow Beasts had erupted and were pouring like molten lava across the land.

"I'll keep an eye on the Beasts," Marina said. "You find the group."

Jax rose. "If you need help, call me."

Marina looked up at him and smiled. "I will."

Jax knelt by her. "Marina, I want you to know something."

"What's that?"

"I'd give my life for you."

Before she could reply, he stood and hurried off to look for the Outcasts. He was eager to find Lynai'seth and the others.

The plateau was broad, dotted with blood-red rocks and deep blue boulders. So far, no signs of the Outcast camp — no carts or small tents.

Jax walked to the middle of the plateau, firmly planted his feet, leaned forward and opened his eyes wide. The plants that Marina fed him had fully restored his sight. Jax was able to see lizards scurrying into holes, twin white butterflies dancing away, an army of bright violet ants crawling single-file into a mound of dirt. Had Marina asked him to count the rocks and pebbles near the eastern edge of the plateau, he could have done so easily.

He moved in a slow, steady circle.

No signs of their friends.

Maybe I didn't understand Lynai'seth's message, Jax thought. *Maybe they're on another ridge ... maybe I have made another big mistake, as usual ...*

Jax ran to the northern corner of the plateau. He gazed out over the landscape at the maze of plateaus, straining his eyes for any signs of Outcasts in the distance — a supply cart, a wisp of campfire smoke, a piece of wet clothing dangling in the breeze ...

Nothing.

His heart sank.

Jax ran to other parts of the plateau, looking out over grand vistas. Aeons ago, this land had been covered in glacial ice — which had melted in the blazing new sun — and sliced the rock, leaving multi-colored mesas that tribes had explored ages ago, then forgot.

Now, there were no signs of life other than bats and birds wheeling in the sky, escaping from Shadow Beasts.

Jax climbed a rock to stand atop the highest point on the plateau.

He stared until his eyes watered.

Please ...

No one.

Anywhere.

Dreadful thoughts crept into his mind — thoughts he had been trying to hold back since finding Lynai'seth's hair band.

Maybe they didn't make it out of the caves.

Maybe they're —

"NO!" he cried. He wouldn't allow the thought to pierce the resolve in his mind, the hope in his heart.

He stood on the rock, a lone figure silhouetted against the setting sun. Jax looked south. Escaping birds seemed to shrink into dots in the sky, then vanish.

He had always loved being able to see great distances, being able to peer into darkest night. Now he found his vision a curse giving him a glimpse into the sprawling emptiness of this life, this world.

The world was so cold, ugly and cruel. It would be so easy to give in to the greater brute power of Antibodies or Shadow Beasts. In the grand scheme of things, what was his contribution? He had failed as a scout for the Outcasts. Who would miss him? His family was gone, his community reduced to rubble. Who would care?

He looked down in the direction of where he had first climbed the plateau to escape Shadow Beasts. Despite the deepening shadows, he saw Marina as if she were bathed in the brightest light. He saw a luminous glow around her.

Marina cares. About everything!

Why couldn't he be more like her — strong and sure? Why hadn't he been born in her Quae Community, where young women and men were fearless?

The fact was that he hadn't, and he had to live with who he was.

Jax again looked at Marina. Something came clear, not only in his vision but also deep in his heart.

He slowly made two fists. His chest tightened. He lifted his head to the setting sun.

Something new burned within him.

He and Marina hadn't come this far only to fail. What was the point in that? He had known loss — all the Outcasts had known loss. Gyro had been able to cobble together a small group of survivors. He had gathered them one by one from fallen communities. He had offered hope where there was none.

Jax knew he could do no less. Even if he and Marina were the last two Outcasts on Dulunae, he would fight with his final breath to keep them alive and get them to safety.

No more stumbling about blindly in caves.

No more feeling sorry for himself or feeling uneasy about the shape of his face, the color of his skin, the size of his large eyes. These were the features that made him who he was. He could view them as handicaps or as strengths.

He suddenly knew that there was a purpose beyond his own limited thoughts and feelings. There was a world outside his mind and heart, where people needed his strength and skill.

Jax returned to Marina's side. "Any luck?" she asked.

"Not yet." He looked over the edge of the plateau. "The Shadow Beasts?"

"As far as I can tell," Marina said, "most of them ran southwest. A few hundred are still down there. Sitting."

"Gyro wanted to head southwest. Dav'yn said southeast. Maybe he was right all along."

"First time I've heard you admit that Dav'yn was right about anything."

"That was my problem, not his." Jax stood. He offered his

hand to Marina. "We're losing light. Let's study the area and find the advantages."

Marina bounced to her feet. "That's what I would have said."

"Marina," Jax said, "the more I act like you, the better I'll be."

She looked at him. Jax leaned, picked up her quarterstaff and handed it to her.

"You know," Marina said, "not everyone can handle the staff. It's been known to burn unfriendly people."

"It kept me alive in the caves."

"It only does that for — special people."

For one special person, according to the customs of our community, she wanted to say.

"Then if there's a way to thank your quarterstaff, please do so," Jax said.

They walked to the southwestern part of the plateau overlooking what had been the entrance to the crystal caves. It was now buried in piles of rock. A handful of Shadow Beasts sniffed around the ruins.

Marina selected the best place to camp, a curving rock that sat slightly higher on the plateau.

"Want to build a fire?" Jax asked.

"No. Might draw unwanted attention."

"It'll get cold tonight."

"We'll — sit near each other," Marina suggested.

Jax smiled. "I'd like that."

The dust from the Shadow Beasts settled. The sun slid behind the western horizon, leaving a blazing red streak of light in its wake. The first stars appeared like pearls on blue velvet cloth.

"I was so sure the Outcasts would be up here," Jax said. "I misunderstood the meaning of the hair band."

"We'll find them," Marina assured.

"Do you think they're —"

" — alive," Marina said firmly. "Our concerns right now are the Beasts. We can't get anywhere if they stay down there below us."

"You think they're all after *us?*"

"Only if we get in their way. I think they're after something more important."

"The Outcasts?"

"Something we can't even guess at."

"Antibodies? We've seen Shadow Beast fighting them."

"I don't know," Marina said. "The Beasts are survivors. They'll help if it suits them — or attack if it suits them as well. We can't be sure what they'll do."

"Some of them are good," Jax said. "A Shadow Beast helped me pull Dav'yn and Feelie from a deep hole."

"Yes, but how do we tell which are good and which are deadly? We can't ask them. They don't have any identifying marks."

Jax thought a moment. "Maybe they're like us — both good *and* bad. Maybe they can choose what they want to be."

"Animals with free will. What will they think of next?" Marina said without a smile.

An uneasy silence passed between them.

"What do we do now?" Jax wondered.

"Have some food and sleep. We have good field position

up here. We'll know if something's coming to attack us."

"That's comforting."

"Right now, it's all we have."

Marina handed Jax the last of the subterranean plants. They ate slowly, savoring every bite.

"Marina," Jax said, gazing at the sky, "do you think we're going to die?"

She was quiet a moment. "Every day."

"Me, too," Jax said. "Do you believe in HayVen?"

"Not if my family isn't in it."

"Me, too. Are you ever scared?"

"Never," Marina said. "Not really. Too busy. How about you?"

Jax grinned. "All the time."

"You seem pretty brave to me."

"I have to be. I hate it. But Gyro made me a scout, so there you have it. I don't look the type. I'm not sure if you've noticed, but I have these big, funny eyes and a round head."

Marina sat closer to him. "I have coarse hair, big ears and a flat nose."

They smiled at each other.

Marina started to say, "We make —"

"— quite a pair," Jax said.

Thin bands of white light appeared in the twilight sky, as if someone were peeking at them from behind a shutter, opened slightly. For a moment, Jax thought he saw a pair of dark eyes forming in the west, staring down at them.

He must have been tired. It had to be a trick.

The sun gave way to waves of pink, red, purple and deep

blue sky. Then night drew over them like a blanket.

A single moon rose over Dulunae. The second moon was hidden.

Moonlight seemed to pour like milk from the night sky onto the plateau, casting everything in a strange shade of chalk.

Jax stirred. He slowly opened his eyes.

For a moment, he feared that he saw a white Shadow Beast. He was about to cry out, but the image disappeared.

Instead, he noticed a white object lodged in a small V-shaped space between two rocks.

"What is it?" Marina asked sleepily.

Jax rose, crossed to the object and held it up in the air.

"Another message from Lynai'seth," he said.

Chapter 24

E lsewhere, in an unknown time and place, a simple dipping process continued.

The mindless ones called Antibodies had invaded communities across Dulunae. They had enslaved the older ones, the Growns, and had left the children to survive on their own, and die.

The brute armies of Antibodies forced the Growns to work in Food Cells below the earth. Here they produced *gnniss,* a pulpy green substance, in large bubbling vats. *Gnniss* weakened the will and strengthened the body.

It prepared the Growns for the dipping.

Gnniss not only strengthened the body but also changed its structure in subtle ways. Aches, pains, diseases, infirmities and maladies all vanished. Wounds healed. Elder Growns felt young again. Younger Growns felt eternal.

The more *gnniss* they ate, the more dependent they became upon the substance.

At the Ripening Time, Growns sated with *gnniss* gladly lined up in the deeper underground realms. They stripped off their work shirts, boots and gloves. One by one, they dipped themselves in a wildly boiling vat of a milky substance called *kleistor.* Their screams were lost in the echoing caverns.

Some did not survive.

Others remained in a half-formed state, part human, part *kleistor.* These creatures, the *nus,* were allowed to slide into underground streams and survive on their own.

A Commander had given these creatures orders to destroy the Two, Marina and Jax, in the caves. *The Two would find the One,* and this was unthinkable.

The *nus* had failed.

They were eliminated.

In a realm without an understandable line of time or three dimensions of space, there was yet another breach, another shudder, a most profound shifting of the order.

CH'NOPS, solid and ancient as a perpetually orbiting planet, rumbled with fury.

The conclusion of this reality was that all the Outcasts would die. This was already known. The continued success of the Outcasts, however, caused a breach in this reality, in this knowledge, allowing for other possibilities and outcomes.

Unacceptable.

This will not happen during the alignment of the two moons.

The dipping of Growns into Antibodies increased.

Meanwhile, a new form of fusion was tested.

Subjects in a remote region of Dulunae had invoked the word CH'NOPS. This usually meant immediate termination. In this case, however, the invoking of CH'NOPS gained them elevation.

The subjects thought that they had discovered the Font on their own. They thought they had surpassed all hope.

They ate exotic fruits and vegetables. They drank a lively concoction of *gnniss.*

They quickly gained strength. Just as quickly, they lost their minds and wills.

The subjects edged into a crystal Font, where there was a

new form of the *kleistor.*

They entered the Font as young humans, as Outcasts, and emerged coated in an impenetrable new substance. They were the forefront of a swift, invincible army, far deadlier than Antibodies.

The subjects no longer had individual names. They were the new breed.

They were the Chitin.

They would easily eliminate the Two — Marina and Jax would soon be dust.

Chapter 25

Gyro was tired.

Tired of the trial and error, rise and fall, joy and sorrow. As he stood before his Outcasts and stared at the two white beasts, he said one thing:

"Enough is enough."

Gyro took off his ceremonial vest, the one all teachers wore in his community. Teachers were the most revered of all people. They occupied the highest positions. There was no greater role imaginable in his community than being in the service of young, questioning minds. Especially orphans.

The Outcasts had called him a "warrior" and many times he had been called upon to fight Antibodies, Shadow Beasts, an endless host of threats. Deep down, he knew he was still a teacher.

And it was time to teach these two white beasts a lesson.

Gyro stepped forward from the group. He craned his neck, the stiff bones popping. He rubbed his shoulders, stretched his arms, made a fist and slapped the fist into his other open hand.

"Okay, dogs," he said, "let's fight."

The white beasts snarled, vile brownish-green ooze dripping from their fangs, their eyes blood-red.

"Wait!"

Lynai'seth stepped forward, sword in hand. "We do this together."

Gyro smiled. "So be it."

S'yen slid on his Battle Gloves, stood next to them and nodded.

The beasts howled.

Terra joined Gyro and the others. "This is crazy, you know. I just came to tell all of you that this is crazy."

"Okay, everyone," Gyro said, "on my count of three, I go left with Terra, Lynai'seth and S'yen go right. One, two —"

"*AVÀTTE! QUΩUN STIYΔ!*" A voice boomed and echoed.

The white beasts continued growling.

The voice seemed to split into two.

"*VTT! QN STY!*"

"*AÀE, UΩU, IΔ!*"

In a billowing roll of smoke, the same smoke Gyro had sensed in the amber canyon, two figures appeared behind the white beasts. The figures slowly approached.

A woman and a man.

The Outcasts couldn't remember the last time they had seen an adult woman or man. All of their families had been destroyed by Antibodies long ago.

The woman and man wore long, simple white robes. They were tall, at least two heads taller than Gyro. The woman wore a loose scarf around her head and neck. The scarf glittered, catching sunlight in hundreds of tiny mirrored disks. It was nearly impossible to see her face. The man wore a silver bird mask with orange plumes. He had bright green hair. He might have been costumed as a G'unk-g'unk.

The Outcasts were speechless. The G'unk-g'unks were motionless. The woman and man stepped next to the huge white beasts and touched them like pets. The woman whispered something, and the beasts seemed to melt into the surrounding rock.

"Any advice on this?" Terra asked Gyro.

"Be ready for anything."

"Now *that's* helpful."

The woman raised a hand. No one understood what she was saying.

"*Cnsnnts thn vwls s th w w spk.*"

The man then said something equally strange: "*Ooa e oe i e ay e ea.*"

The woman continued in a string of indecipherable sounds, some issuing from the depths of her throat, others from the upper parts of her nasal passage. The Outcasts couldn't tell if she was speaking or singing. They couldn't decide if she was happy or angry.

The man's words were not as sharp and crisp as the woman's. His seemed more rounded, somewhat more melodious.

"Xalid!" Gyro called over his shoulder.

Xalid struggled but could not pick out a single word from their garbled language.

"Maybe they're crazy people speaking gibberish," he decided.

The Outcasts had come from more than forty communities throughout Dulunae. Not one of them recognized what the woman and man were saying.

The woman and man grew frustrated. They turned away.

"We failed their test, and we don't even know the rules!" Terra said.

Suddenly Yan jerked his head, as if lifting out of a deep trance. He stepped forward.

"*Y spk th cmmn tng, ou ea e oo oue,*" he said.

The woman nodded. "*Ys.*"

The man grinned. "*E.*"

They reached out and took each other's hands. They spoke, not exactly at the same time but as if rapidly completing each other's words: "Consonants, then vowels, is the way we speak."

"They're speaking the Common Tongue!" Terra said. Xalid laughed.

"Of course," the woman and man said together. "That's the easiest language we ever created — eleven major consonants and eleven vowels dancing together. We've taught desert monkeys to speak the Common Tongue. We speak at least 5,279 languages." They laughed. "We're studying the final 5,280[th]."

Gyro stepped forward. "Who are you?"

The woman turned her head a bit, her face still winking with reflected light from her scarf. Together she and the man said: "I am H'Êshra, and I am Ma'h'bri."

"Who is who?"

The man pointed to the woman. Together, they said, "This one is H'Êshra."

"So, the woman is H'Êshra, and the man is Ma'h'bri," Gyro told the Outcasts. For a moment, he could savor being a teacher again.

"You are the Ones?" the woman and man asked them.

"The Ones who what?" Terra asked.

"The Ones."

"Do we win a prize?"

"You are Terra," H'Êshra and Ma'h'bri said, both smiling.

"How do you know?'

"The funny healer," they said.

"KLEISTOR!" Yan shouted.

"That's Yan," Terra said. "He's funny, too."

"The interpreter."

H'Êshra and Ma'h'bri spoke to each other in ten, perhaps twenty languages. They looked at Gyro. "You are not all here," they said.

"No," Gyro admitted. "We lost our two scouts, Marina and Jax. And a group of five broke ranks and went their own direction."

H'Êshra and Ma'h'bri again spoke to each other in a variety of languages. "You lost the Two," they said to Gyro.

"In the crystal caves," Gyro said. "They were scouting for us. Then there was an attack of Shadow Beasts, so we had to break camp and take to higher ground."

"Shadow Beasts …"

"We were about to look for Marina and Jax, but there was an earthquake. An avalanche closed the cave. We needed to move on to safety. That's when we saw the G'unk-g'unks."

"G'unk-g'unks." H'Êshra and Ma'h'bri crossed to the first cart and petted the birds.

"Do you know these creatures?" Gyro asked.

H'Êshra and Ma'h'bri nodded. "Our histories are common, ancient and deep. They sensed your trouble and came for you during their forced migration."

Terra laughed. "And here we thought that we had tamed *them.*"

"Hardly. They are far more advanced than any of us."

"They attacked us," Gyro noted.

H'Êshra and Ma'h'bri turned to him. "Did you strike at them first?"

Gyro nodded. "We tried herding them, but Dav'yn drew his knife."

"They simply defended themselves."

"Ru'an was right about these creatures," Lynai'seth said under her breath.

"A volunteer gave its life so that you could explore the mysteries of healing," H'Êshra and Ma'h'bri said. "You have two members of the Avian Community, do you not?"

"Yes," Gyro said, "S'yen and Ru'an."

"They know the value of the sacrifice. You have done well, Gyro," H'Êshra and Ma'h'bri said.

"Is this HayVen?"

H'Êshra and Ma'h'bri smiled at each other. "No, it is not. At least not to outsiders."

"Does HayVen exist?"

The question had been in the minds and hearts of the Outcasts for so long. It seemed to hover in the air like a thing come to life.

They all listened carefully for the answer.

"Oh, yes, HayVen exists," H'Êshra and Ma'h'bri said. "It goes by many names. It takes on many forms. But it certainly exists."

"How do we find it?"

"Come," H'Êshra and Ma'h'bri said. "You look tired and hungry. Free the creatures you call G'unk-g'unks. They have fulfilled their duty and must continue on their mission. Let the children play. We have fountains of sparkling waters, filled with glorious rainbows. We will serve you bountiful meals of fruits and vegetables, milk and honey."

"*Kleistor!*" Yan again cried.

Gyro turned to H'Êshra and Ma'h'bri. "Can you explain what he means by that word?"

H'Êshra broke into her language of consonants; Ma'h'bri responded to her in vowels. They spoke so rapidly that not even Xalid could assemble the consonants and vowels into understandable words.

"We will explain all in the fullness of time," they said. "Please join us."

Gyro and the others removed harnesses from the G'unk-g'unks. S'yen and Ru'an bowed, thanked them, and said farewell to the noble animals. The giant birds bowed in return, made their familiar cry of "*gunk, gunk,*" and scurried away.

H'Êshra and Ma'h'bri led the Outcasts through a dim passageway to a magnificent courtyard encircled in lush blue-green trees, thick yellow bushes, a rainbow array of wildflowers and assortment of fountains spouting many colors. Small pileated birds with green feathers and white wings darted through the trees.

Crimson squirrels bounded from tree to bush. Fish the color of a blazing orange sunset wriggled through the water in the fountains, through a small stream that criss-crossed the courtyard. The courtyard itself was tiled in bright blues, reds and whites. The patterns of the tiling had a hypnotic effect.

The courtyard led to a large house the color of sand. There were archways, stairways, balconies, flower boxes, cascades of blue-and-violet ivy, all piecing together in unusual angles that seemed to defy logic. It looked as if a person could walk up a staircase past a balcony, continue along the staircase and stand upside-down from the originating point.

Amber towers and turrets loomed over the house. Thick white clouds passed so rapidly above the towers that it seemed that the clouds were stationary and the towers were sliding through space, like the masts of a ship on a boundless blue sea.

H'Êshra and Ma'h'bri seemed to be talking to a large tree. The two guardian creatures appeared for a moment in the shade of the tree.

"Tell us what those white beasts are," Lynai'seth demanded. "I've seen them before — many times."

"Of course you have, dear child," H'Êshra and Ma'h'bri said, "you are blessed with the Sight. Not like your friend, Yan's, but a different Sight. You are missing three hair bands. A noble sacrifice and clever way to bring the Two here. Might we touch the fourth hair band?"

"Why?"

"Our 'white beasts,' as you say — the *caeenri-beda* — can track the scent of the cloth."

Lynai'seth was reluctant to part with a hair ribbon.

"Explain."

"Dear, there is no time," H'Êshra and Ma'h'bri said. "The Shadow Beasts are upon the land. Their number is legion.

Your friends will never find this place alone."

"You mean they're alive?"

"That remains to be seen."

"How do you know?"

"Because we are Knowers."

"Knowers?" Gyro said, astonished.

H'Êshra and Ma'h'bri nodded. "The last of our kind. Once again, Gyro, you have found the last survivors of a dying community."

"How — why —"

"We shall explain. Now, though, we must send the *caeenribeda* to save your friends before they die." H'Êshra and Ma'h'bri turned to Lynai'seth. "May we see the hair band?"

Lynai'seth turned to Gyro for advice. "Your choice," he said. "I stand behind it."

"Terra?" Lynai'seth said.

"Do it," Terra replied. "We got here safely. The white beasts never attacked us. The Knowers are people of learning and peace."

Lynai'seth pondered. *If there is any chance I can save Jax ... and Marina ...*

She quickly unfastened the fourth hair band. "I left one in the cave, one on the plateau, and one by the river for them to follow."

Terra looked at the hair band. "But it's in your native language. They can't read it."

"Jax can. Klanga saw to that."

"Klanga?"

"I asked her to teach Jax."

"Why didn't *you* teach him?"

"I was observing my Period of Silence. Talking to one of his kind ..." her voice trailed off. "By my customs, I wasn't permitted to speak to him for a time. But I can always speak with children."

"So you bent the rules a little to communicate with Jax," Terra said with a grin.

Lynai'seth did not respond. She handed the hair band to H'Êshra and Ma'h'bri. "How exquisite!" they cried. "The glorious joining of art and language! We have never touched Shi'vaal cloth ... until now!"

They gestured to the two white beasts. The *caeenri-beda* sniffed the hair bands, then vanished.

Lynai'seth snatched back the hair band and slid it onto one of her long braids.

"Child," H'Êshra and Ma'h'bri said to her, "you are a living library. A history."

"Of a lost community," she said.

"Nothing is ever lost. Only placed elsewhere."

"What does that mean?"

"So many questions! The future is in good hands."

"You play too many games, H'Êshra and Ma'h'bri."

"You are much like our granddaughter," they said. "She never liked games, either."

"Where is this wise child now?"

H'Êshra and Ma'h'bri paused and lowered their heads. "Gone. Like so many others."

"I'm ... I'm sorry," Lynai'seth said.

"Thank you, child. But let us look to the future. We can

help answer many of your questions, with a touch. Now let the children go play in the crystal Fonts," they said. "They will enjoy the colored waters."

Gyro gave an order which was passed along to the others. The children needed no extra urging to run and play. They jumped into the fountains and splashed each other and shrieked merrily.

H'Êshra and Ma'h'bri crossed to a multi-levelled building surrounded with looming statues of birds, dogs, lions, horses, fish, rabbits and lizards. The animals rested atop pillars etched with strange languages. H'Êshra gazed up at a large iron door adorned with brass and pewter inscriptions. She raised her right index finger and touched a small elliptical space on the door.

The door swung open. Radiant light flooded from the inner room.

The Outcasts gasped in awe.

Chapter 26

"Welcome to the Font of Knowledge," H'Êshra and Ma'h'bri said with pride.

Gyro, Lynai'seth, S'yen, Terra, Yan, Xalid and some of the others cautiously entered the great hall. The ceiling was so high and distant, the sunlight so blindingly powerful that at first the hall seemed to rise endlessly to the sky. Once their vision adjusted, the Outcasts could see paintings of sky and clouds, the twin moons of Dulunae and star formations — an entire charting of the heavens on the distant ceiling.

The levels within the Font were as ornate and complicated as the many terraces and walkways they had already seen outside. There were steps, balconies, walkways, tiers, archways, tunnels and flat tiled paths that wove through countless sculptures, books, paintings, costumes, fabrics, furnishings, tools, weapons and armor.

The Outcasts saw books with metallic covers, cloth, leather, paper, wood, bone and even rock. Terra leaned towards a huge glass globe in which letters of a strange alphabet floated like living creatures, organizing and reorganizing.

"They *are* fish," H'Êshra and Ma'h'bri said, anticipating her question. "They are a living language. They bid you welcome."

"Tell them I send my kindest regards," Terra replied.

"The languages," Xalid said softly. "So many cultures, dialects, vocal patterns. So many ways to communicate … a thousand-thousand ways to say the word *love*. Words spoken, words written, words lost, words found …"

Lynai'seth smiled like one of the children. "Can we — read about our own communities here?"

"You will find the sum of all that the Knowers have discovered through the ages," H'Êshra and Ma'h'bri said.
Yan walked to the middle of the floor, stood in a circle of light, dropped to his knees and cried tears of joy.

Gyro walked to a marble pillar. Behind it stood a statue of an Antibody.

"This looks familiar," he said.

H'Êshra and Ma'h'bri joined him. "As well it should. You would not be here, had you not found the Seven in the wastelands."

Gyro studied it. "The Seven Statues."

"Statues? Child, the creatures you found in the wastelands were true Antibodies."

Gyro turned to them sharply.

"*Dead* Antibodies?"

"Not dead as we term it. Petrified. The *kleistor* in their forms hardened."

"*Kleistor!*" Yan cried.

"It is one of the substances from which the Antibodies are created," H'Êshra and Ma'h'bri said. "We of the Knowers built the ring of Seven Antibodies as an outpost. It serves as a guide for those who seek truth, as is your case. It also serves as a mighty weapon, offering the Seven-Character Word as a defense against Antibodies. You found each letter at the base of the — statues, as you call them."

"You mean CH'N—" Gyro began to say.

H'Êshra and Ma'h'bri raised their hands quickly to

interrupt him. "Do NOT speak the word lightly! It brings down destruction. It is the fire of darkness. Even to utter its name is to accept its will. It knows the power of language. That is why it has destroyed communities and left our Knowers for dead. We are the only two Knowers left in this life, Gyro, unless …"

"Unless what?"

"Unless you join us and become Knowers, too. We can begin a new community. Now. We have been hoping for children to walk amongst us. We have been waiting for you, Gyro, Lynai'seth, Yan, Xalid, S'yen — all of you."

Gyro was suspicious. "Then why didn't you send someone to help us? Why all the dark mysteries and puzzles? Do you know the danger we've faced? I've lost my scouts! The loss of one person is unacceptable. The loss of two is unthinkable!"

"We cannot leave this place," H'Êshra and Ma'h'bri said. "We are its final protectors. The ring of Seven Antibodies we built in the wastelands was our final act outside these hallowed grounds. We are old and weak and tired. Our time has passed. You can restore this Font of Knowledge to life."

"Are we safe here? What about the Shadow Beasts? Are they good or deadly?"

"They are good … and deadly."

Gyro's skin tone turned a deep red. "Stop playing games!"

"They are both. We need to observe and decide how one is different from another."

"That shouldn't be difficult."

"Oh? Can you tell a good human from a bad one simply

by looking?"

"No …"

"We draw close to uncovering the mystery of the Shadow Beasts but do not have the answer yet. We do not know from whence they came, why they exist or what their mission is. Perhaps, as the new breed of Knowers, the *Congnosci,* you can find the answers before all is lost."

"What will it take to become a Knower?" Xalid asked excitedly.

H'Êshra and Ma'h'bri spoke to each other in a collision of languages, then turned to the others. "One thing."

Xalid's eyes widened. "What thing?"

H'Êshra and Ma'h'bri raised their right index fingers and pointed to the ceiling of the great hall. "To gain access to this Font of Knowledge, we all have the marking on our right finger. It is a tiny incision. You saw how we opened the great metal door. Receiving the marking on your finger indicates your agreement, your contract with the great history of Knowers. Will you join us?"

Xalid smiled. "Yes." He raised his right finger in the air in imitation of H'Êshra and Ma'h'bri.

Yan also raised a finger.

Some of the others also held up a finger.

Gyro did not.

Nor did Lynai'seth, Terra or S'yen.

"Some of you doubt us," H'Êshra and Ma'h'bri said. "We hoped, Gyro, that as a teacher, you of all people would thirst for the knowledge contained in these chambers. Perhaps you should know that once we leave this Font of Knowledge, only those with the marking can reenter. Others are forbidden a second visit. Look around before you decide. Find the history of your community and celebrate it with us. Then we will have a feast together."

Lynai'seth studied them. She turned to Gyro. "We should give this a chance. We may learn something." She wandered off under a brass archway that had inscriptions resembling the language on her garment.

"I agree," Terra said, tapping her finger on the globe of living language-fish.

Gyro turned. H'Êshra and Ma'h'bri had disappeared.

As had everyone else.

He reluctantly joined the others in examining books, records, maps, garments and tools. He climbed ladders and crossed bridges. Each time he entered a small chamber, a shutter on a window would shift, allowing sunlight to pour onto him and cool breezes to waft across his face. When he drew near a small fountain, crystal water would begin to trickle.

Everything H'Êshra and Ma'h'bri said *seemed* to be true, but Gyro still felt as if they were holding back information. In his community, there were two ways to be deceitful: to openly tell a lie or to silently withhold the truth. Either way was dangerous.

They knew about Antibodies, Shadow Beasts and the Seven-Character Word. They knew about the Outcasts. Were they a higher intelligence he couldn't understand with his own limited knowledge, or were they a higher level of danger?

Aren't people of knowledge — the Knowers — supposed to be honest?

Gyro climbed on a spiralling wooden staircase to a higher level of the Font of Knowledge. It had no railing or supporting beams but stood firmly.

For now, his Outcasts were healthy, well fed and safe. He could hear the children playing in the fountains outside, their laughter rising joyously to the sky. This was the closest thing to HayVen he could imagine. As he gazed up at the paintings on the ceiling, he believed — for a moment — that this *could* be HayVen.

He heard Yan's voice echoing excitedly in the multitude of passageways. Yan had been considered the dreamer, the boy lost to his own fantasy world, but Gyro had often relied on his insight. They still had not found the "angles of rainbows" that Yan had referred to so long ago, but he had been right about the word *kleistor* as an ominous piece of this vast puzzle. H'Êshra and Ma'h'bri had verified this.

Gyro had always wished that Yan could speak in more coherent forms, sentences rather than words, so that his thoughts took on fuller meaning. As he listened to Yan cry out in the halls of this vast Font of Knowledge, he felt as if his wish were coming true. Gyro realized that Yan was speaking — laughing — in long sentences and full paragraphs.

Xalid was running from room to room as if trying to absorb everything at the same time. Lynai'seth appeared in a pool of white light, looking like a princess from a distant realm where all things were good. Terra was still gazing at the fishbowl. She looked up at Gyro, smiled and waved.

Gyro wished with all his heart that Marina and Jax would walk through the door. Marina could have found a mural recounting the seashore history of her Quae Community. Jax could have seen the portraits of great leaders from his Kerta Community.

Gyro turned a corner and froze. Shutters opened. Sunlight bounced off a tall glass display containing dazzling scarves, intricate blankets and thick rugs from the village of his betrothed, Calyssta Saine Ty. A folk song that Calyssta herself might have sung seemed to curl from the shadows and stroke his ears.

Had the world been different, he would have married her in a few Sun Cycles, they would have opened their school for orphans, they would have lived a happy life close to their families.

Things weren't supposed to turn out the way they have —

Now there was a brute world, destruction. Antibodies. Shadow Beasts and other monsters.

Loss — of families, friends, homes, communities, Jax and Marina.

Other losses — Dav'yn, Kon-gor, S'h'ta, Cobin-4 and Bayne, who had raced off to their own dark destinies.

Wait —

An insight skimmed the edge of his thoughts like one of the fish Terra was so keenly observing. Gyro raced up and down ladders and stairways. He looked at exhibits, displays, dioramas, maps, history tomes and geography books. He darted under archways, climbed tiers and slammed to a halt at an open book of Dulunae beautifully scripted on parchment.

The Knowers had amassed the remnants of ravaged communities. They had collected artifacts from the very communities that Antibodies had raided.

Only Gyro had gathered survivors from each of more

than forty communities. Only he knew what the Knowers had done.

Were they simply explorers, seekers of knowledge? Did they somehow know where and when Antibodies would strike, then follow them after an attack?

Were the Knowers in league with the Antibodies?

Gyro's skin turned a sick green at the thought.

Despite their bright kindnesses and hopeful words, he would remain as guarded and cautious as if he were approaching two poisonous snakes.

***

The Outcasts gathered around a wide, round marble table. Each place was set with a crystal glass of water, finger bowl, plate, napkin and gleaming silverware.

H'Êshra and Ma'h'bri entered the dining hall. H'Êshra wore an iridescent purple-and-black garment that shimmered like a fantastic liquid in moonlight. She again wore a scarf of tiny mirrors that hid her face. When she leaned into candlelight, the scarf fell away from her cheek for a moment, and she suddenly seemed quite beautiful.

Ma'h'bri appeared taller and more imposing than ever, his hair now thick and white. He no longer wore a silver mask. He had violet eyes that seemed wise and kind. His face was a friendly pumpkin color.

They stood near the round table and greeted the Outcasts. The children looked clean, their hair brushed and hands scrubbed to glowing perfection. Kg was able to control his body and sit with Zwyna, Mohir'a'qest, Tu'ghee T'an, Lhista T'an and Ru'an. Klanga held Feelie on her lap. Oolo sat at the table. He could not speak or move much, but he was able to eat his meal.

H'Êshra and Ma'h'bri sat between Gyro and Lynai'seth. They whistled in an elaborate sequence and looked up to the rafters. Circle-formations of silver birds descended bearing trays in their beaks. The trays were filled with cherries, oranges, bananas, apples, pineapples and fruits from a variety of Dulunae Communities. Red birds swooped with baskets of bread. Three ivory-colored kangaroos brought carafes of water stored in their pouches.

The Outcasts laughed as animals darted back and forth or lumbered about serving water, bread, fruit and vegetables.

"How can animals do this?" Lynai'seth asked.

H'Êshra and Ma'h'bri smiled. "They are not merely animals, my dear. They are brilliant creatures who have remained loyal to the Knowers. We have lost much through the ages, but not our friends."

"Are the G'unk-g'unks your friends?" Ru'an asked across the great table.

H'Êshra and Ma'h'bri nodded. "Indeed. Long ago, the Knowers found an ancient breed of G'unk-g'unks under attack in the desert. Our people fought side-by-side until the enemy was defeated."

"Which enemy?" Gyro wondered.

H'Êshra and Ma'h'bri grew silent. They offered more bread to Lynai'seth.

They're hiding something, Gyro thought.

Red-and-black spotted monkeys gathered glasses and dishes as more kangaroos appeared. Even S'yen, who never seemed to smile, bore a grin on his face.

The dining hall echoed with the rattle and clatter of plates, glasses and silverware, with the sound of light conversation, joking and laughter. Gyro kept watching the shadows under the archways, suspicious of a sneak attack from an unknown enemy.

The meal progressed without any attack.

Five green camels appeared. White apes jumped from the camels and served sweet desserts, cakes, cookies and pastries thick with white filling that made the children squeal with delight.

Still no attack.

After the meal, the children wandered under a starry sky to their sleeping quarters. Each Outcast had his or her own bed with a thick mattress and a thick, warm blanket.

H'Êshra and Ma'h'bri asked Gyro, Lynai'seth, Terra and S'yen to join them by a small fire in one of the courtyards.

H'Êshra and Ma'h'bri spoke softly. "Gyro, we sense your distrust. You have skin colors that betray you."

Gyro had to laugh. "I know. It's a burden. Fortunately, most people don't know what the colors mean, so they can't tell my thoughts or moods."

"That's what you think," Terra said.

"You believe we are scavengers preying upon the death and destruction the Antibodies leave," H'Êshra and Ma'h'bri said.

Gyro looked at them. "Yes."

"You feel we may be working with them."

"Yes."

"This is good in a leader. You do not distrust. You exhibit wisdom. Our ancestors trusted everyone and all things, and we fell because of it. Our ancestors were able to save the G'unk-g'unks many Sun Cycles ago, but they could not save themselves. They trusted certain desert tribes, which proved fatal."

"You are not telling us everything," Gyro said, firelight flickering on his strong face.

H'Êshra and Ma'h'bri leaned towards the fire, stoking it with long sticks. Sparks leapt before them. Crickets chirped in the darkness. "The Community of Knowers is — was — an ancient one. The Font of Knowledge is our final museum and library, where we have amassed our discoveries. We had Fonts of Knowledge across Dulunae, in remote, snowy mountain villages, in distant hogans, in sun-washed valleys and deep, stark deserts. No more."

"What happened?" Lynai'seth asked. "Antibodies?"

"They are the latest manifestation of a greater power," H'Êshra and Ma'h'bri said.

"Do you mean the Seven-Character Name?" Gyro asked.

H'Êshra nodded. Ma'h'bri gazed into the fire.

"The sudden migration of the G'unk-g'unks marks the beginning of the end," they said.

Terra frowned. "What do you mean?"

"Watch the animals to know your world. When crickets and frogs grow silent, a river is dying. When fireflies vanish, a stream and its plants are dying. When butterflies disappear, the plants are lost. Small birds detect changes in climate, in air, in caves. If you want to see the immediate future, watch the animals."

Gyro glanced at birds flying into the dark boughs of nearby trees.

"The G'unk-g'unks are smart, tame and wise creatures," H'Êshra and Ma'h'bri continued. "They would not run unless there was immediate danger approaching. Our white beasts, the *caeenri-beda,* have followed your journey. We can communicate with them, and they have said that other creatures are migrating southwest, in this direction. They flee approaching doom."

Lynai'seth shifted uneasily. "Doom? How can anything be worse than what we've experienced?"

"You Outcasts represent hope," H'Êshra and Ma'h'bri said. "You are the opposite of the Seven-Character Name."

"What is the secret of this Seven-Character Word?" Gyro asked sharply. "We used the word against Antibodies in the desert, and the Antibodies froze in their tracks."

"Gyro," H'Êshra and Ma'h'bri said, "you are the only ones who have ever deciphered the mystery of the Seven."

"Lynai'seth and Yan figured it out."

"You have gathered children from dying communities and formed a common goal. You are the hope, the promise. You work together. You solve the mystery and you endure all hardship. Your greatest tests are to come. The Seven-Character Word wants you."

"Wants us dead?"

"Worse — wants you alive in a slave state."

"Are we safe here?"

"No. There is no safe place but HayVen." H'Êshra and Ma'h'bri stoked the fire again. The sparks shot into the air, drifted, faded in the night. "Our people have studied many cultures, many communities, many mythologies and beliefs and languages. The communities number like the stars, yet are as wonderfully unique as the imprints on your fingertips. We have learned a great secret through the ages — we have learned that no matter how diverse our cultures are through-out all history, they all refer to the One in their lore. This includes all of your Outcast Communities."

Gyro thought. "My family talked about *aaifiaa,* the one passage to a safe place."

Terra nodded. "Ours is One Healer."

"My Shi'vaal Community discussed One Silence," Lynai'seth said.

S'yen somehow understood all that H'Êshra and Ma'h'bri said. He locked his thumbs together and wiggled his fingers as if they were a bird's wings, indicating One Flight.

"So what is the One?" Gyro asked. "A human, an animal, a place, a way of silence, a language, a form of art?"

"We do not know," H'Êshra and Ma'h'bri said. "We have narrowed the possibilities to one of two hundred. We need more time. Your friend Yan can help. As can Xalid and some of the others."

"Why should we help you?"

"Our studies indicate *the Two will find the One.* We believe that your scouts, Marina and Jax, are the Two."

"Two what?" Gyro cried.

Lynai'seth felt a warmth in her heart, as if their words had joined with the fire and had brightened the dark and cold.

Terra jumped. "I feel something," she said. "It feels like Jax and Marina are — alive."

Gyro turned to her. "Are you sure?"

"As sure as I feel the pain of my patients."

S'yen nodded.

In a world of uncertainties, Gyro also felt a balance, a rightness in the statement that his scouts were alive. He jumped to his feet. "Let's bring them in here!"

"We have sent the *caeenri-beda*," H'Êshra and Ma'h'bri said. "As Lynai'seth knows, they are brilliant trackers."

"I can send a team," Gyro said. "We're rested and fed. We're ready."

"You cannot move the way the *caeenri-beda* can. They can fold into shadows, into water, into the wind itself."

"So we sit and wait for them?" Gyro said.

"We return to the Font of Knowledge to learn who or what the One is," H'Êshra and Ma'h'bri said. "I fear we have no time left. The migrating G'unk-g'unks are the first sign that all is lost."

"You still want us to mark our fingers to gain passage to the Font of Knowledge?" Gyro said. "I refuse. My community forbids such markings, and I still honor my community."

"I have the markings of my Shi'vaal Community," Lynai'seth said. "I can add no more."

"I'm against any more cuts or incisions than a person needs in life," Terra said.

H'Êshra and Ma'h'bri stood. "So be it. Yan and Xalid have said they would join us. The rest of you can wait on our word."

Gyro sent Lynai'seth to summon Yan and Xalid. Their eyes were aglow in the campfire light as H'Êshra and Ma'h'bri explained to them in their native tongues what was about to happen. They would receive small cuts in their right fingers. H'Êshra would embed a tiny ceramic piece etched with thousands of minute characters. Then Ma'h'bri would seal the incisions with stitching and ointments. The embedded ceramic piece would fit exactly with the small ellipse on the door of the Font of Knowledge, unlocking it.

While H'Êshra and Ma'h'bri administered the ceramic pieces to Xalid and Yan, Gyro walked through the courtyard with Terra and Lynai'seth. "I can't stay here and do nothing while Jax and Marina are out there in the wild," he said.

"If they are," Terra said, "we have no idea where exactly they might be."

"The *caeenri-beda* are good trackers," Lynai'seth said. "I saw them follow us while we travelled with the G'unk-g'unks. If anything, I've learned how smart and powerful these new creatures are."

Gyro rubbed his chin. "What is this about Jax and Marina being the Two? The Two what? And who or what is the One?"

"Let's hope Yan and Xalid find out," Terra said.

"I hate riddles. I want answers."

"That's the teacher in you. You feel the need to be in control."

"We've gotten this far," Gyro said. "I want to make sure we all reach HayVen safely."

"I have to check on Oolo's hand," Terra said. "You two discuss this." She wandered off towards the sleeping quarters.

Gyro looked at Lynai'seth. She seemed a perfect part of the starry night sky, the quiet fountains, the secret gardens and tiled villas. "H'Êshra and Ma'h'bri say you are blessed with the Sight. What did they mean?"

"I have no idea," she said. "I have no special abilities."

"You sing in a way that calms everyone."

"Any child can do that in my community. I lived a life separate from the rest of the young people in my land. I was told I was exceptional, but I always felt inferior. Different. Quite shy."

"You didn't seem shy taming the G'unk-g'unks."

Lynai'seth smiled a bit. "I thought about what Jax might do in the same situation. He would have been terrified, but he also would have leapt onto the bird. He always places the needs of others higher than his own. I learn from him."

"Do you love him?"

Lynai'seth paused, lost in thought. "The word has thousands of meanings," she finally said. "I honor him in mind and heart — more than I thought I would."

Gyro smiled. "He would love hearing that. He has high regard for you."

"You speak as if he's still alive. Do you believe so?"

"I hope so."

Light pulsed in the distant sky, to the northeast. Lynai'seth excused herself, and Gyro remained outside, with the night, with his thoughts and worries. He looked over his shoulder at the Font of Knowledge. Lights burned brightly within the chambers.

Time passed subtly and gently, like a midnight stream.

In the deepest ravine of night and sleep, there was a shift in the wind. A scent both subtle and strong, like jasmine, drifted.

Gyro was dozing on a cement bench near a fountain. He stirred.

The wind, soft as the touch of a finger, moved through the trees, bushes and deep night flowers.

Gyro inhaled.

He awoke.

He had experienced a thousand new aromas and scents in the home of H'Êshra and Ma'h'bri. Nothing like this.

Gyro sat up and breathed deeply. He leaned, shut his eyes and inhaled deeply again.

Smoke.

Burning wood.

Dust storm.

Electric air.

Gyro stood.

The wind spoke to him in a whisper.

It was an odor he could not describe but could never forget.

Shadow Beasts.

Chapter 27

I n the place without a name, in a time without measure, the raging grew louder. Dark corners erupted in fiery white lava flows and billowing black clouds of smoke. Crystal streams turned putrid green, overflowing on the delicate white streaks and serene diamond shapes that represented a tranquil order.

On Dulunae, a place with measure, a world passing through time from beginning to end, the deep caves burned furiously. Lines of *gnniss*-filled slaves leapt into seething vats of *kleistor*. Many of the slaves had yet to reach the Ripening. It did not matter. Time was of the essence.

There were crying failures in the bubbling vats. And screaming successes. And those who emerged as part human, part *kleistor*. This breed of the *nus* could be exploited as spies in deep, dark rivers.

The new Antibodies streamed from the world below to passageways leading above ground. They moved under one will, not their own. They served a single purpose. They burst from hidden earth through mounds of rock and spilled forth across ravaged land, spreading like disease. Their dark hearts could be seen from a distance through their milky, transparent skin, pulsing in steady rhythm.

All the while, the Chitin tested their invulnerable new bodies as they crossed the desert wastelands. They jumped from high rocks and slammed to the ground. Then rose, unharmed. They crept. They stood. They ran.

They will fall as drops of rain from the sky; they will number as grains of sand upon the shore …

These new armies were converging on a single point, a place those old fools, the Knowers, quaintly called the Font of Knowledge. More a Font of Folly, the last museum on Dulunae to capture information from all communities, all histories, and offer clues to the past, the present and the future of Dulunae.

The Antibodies — and Chitin — had a final mission.

The Two are about to discover the One.

Stop them —

Chapter 28

The winds of Dulunae spoke their own language, as softly as a flowered scent, as loudly as a raging storm. The winds foretold rain for parched lands, predicted hot, burning skies or bitter, piercing snow and ice.

Insects, plants and animals listened to the wind, in their way. Humans did not. Humans waited until the last moment, looked up and saw a rainstorm. Then ran for cover.

People from Marina's Quae Community had come to know the wind, its power to fill a sail on a ship, to destroy the sturdiest vessel at sea. People from Jax's Kerta Community had come to know the scent of the soil, the way the earth breathed air, the small gasp emitted when vegetables were plucked from rich, wet farmland.

The two communities knew the beginning and end of the wind, from its humble birth in rich crops to its death in the high seas.

The wind spoke to Gyro as he stood in the courtyard by the Font of Knowledge. He tried understanding its message but failed. His keen ability to smell was lost to his thoughts as he tried sorting out the hundreds of scents he detected on the wind.

He stood in the courtyard. The wind moved on.

This was a gust like no other, filled with smoke as Gyro had guessed, burning wood, dust, electric air, thousands of animals, the smell of Shadow Beasts, the manufactured odor of Antibodies, the putrid stench of Chitin. The wind had its own character, a monstrous life that was greater than the sum of its many horrid parts.

The wind fought with itself, the monstrous odors at war with the fragrances of the trees, bushes, flowers and fountains surrounding the Font of Knowledge. In this whirl of wind, two threads of sweet breeze slipped away and found one small opening in the Font.

In the rafters, two doves stirred as the twin breezes slipped past them. The tiny winds curled downward, toward a great book open on a wooden display. The doves followed the winds down towards the book.

In their final effort, the twin breezes slapped the flame of a pair of guttering candles. The candlelight flickered, wavering like a mad pair of human hands. The doves seemed to take this as a signal. They flapped their wings until a single page in the book lifted gently, like the wing of a butterfly, and settled.

A human entered the chamber and clapped his hands with joy. The noise startled the doves, and they flew away. Candlelight fell on the new page in the book.

A glass bowl reflected an arc of the candlelight on its curved surface.

The living language of colored fish in the glass bowl, the creatures that had so intrigued Terra, had been sleeping. The shifting candlelight awoke them. Before the candles sputtered and died, the fish saw —

Words on the new page in the book.

A final clue —

The candles died. Darkness returned like a pressing hand.

The fish were electric and alive.

They darted about in the glass bowl. The fish swam rapidly, almost violently, to attract attention. The two Outcasts, Yan and Xalid, were still in the Font of Knowledge. Xalid was on one of the higher levels, translating an ancient epic tale. Yan was near the fish. He glanced at them while passing by the globe but did not pay attention. He clapped his hands again as if about to eat a fantastic meal. This Font of Knowledge was a feast beyond his wildest dreams. He wasn't sure where to look first.

The fish had signalled for Yan to bring Terra the Healer — *she* would understand them.

Yan turned away. Their urgent message was lost in the gloom of a darkened hallway.

The fish darted back and forth to the point of exhaustion. Wild chatter, arguments, and final communication took place among them. A decision. Two of the fish swam in tight circles. The others swam furiously, zigzagging in elaborate patterns.

As Yan turned towards them, a single golden fish shot from the watery glass globe, arched through the air and fell on the book, on the new page, on the new words. It had seconds to live. Its tiny body pulsed, flickered. Its lips gasped for water.

It slowed.

Yan looked.

He stared for a moment as if in a trance, as if his mind were far away. He blinked, shook his head and realized that a small fish had somehow leapt from the globe and was dying. He scooped the tiny creature into his hand and carefully placed it back into the glass bowl. The fish sank. Stopped. Flickered. Revived.

Yan looked at the place in the book where the fish had fallen. He stared, and his eyes widened as he read. Yan rarely paid attention to the present moment, rarely spoke words relating to the present, but now a single urgent cry escaped his lips.

"XALID!"

In a blink, his friend responded, running down staircases, under archways, across walkways and jumping to the floor. Yan pointed to the book.

The two of them found one sentence.

Xalid ran off to find H'Êshra and Ma'h'bri, who were lost in the maze of books and museum pieces. He called out in a series of consonants, then vowels, using the Common Tongue. He heard them reply, but their voices were distant.

Xalid climbed ladders and raced across tiled passageways. He found them in a weak circle of candlelight. Ma'h'bri was resting in the crook of H'Êshra's shoulder. She spoke in Xalid's native tongue and said, "He is exhausted. He fears we have failed you …"

Ma'h'bri's eyes were shut, his pumpkin skin a sick brown color in the candlelight.

"We found something," Xalid said. "We need you now."

"I will not leave Ma'h'bri," H'Êshra replied. She stroked his forehead.

"Then I'll help you with him." Xalid slid his arm around Ma'h'bri and lifted him. Ma'h'bri was tall, but thin and light.

H'Êshra led the way through the Font of Knowledge. By now, birds were flying through the Font, monkeys chattering, kangaroos lurching through the dark hallways. H'Êshra came to a bright mirror and stepped right through it without pausing. Xalid followed with Ma'h'bri.

They were suddenly crossing the main level to Yan and the fish. Yan's fingers were speeding across the page. The message was close, so close …

H'Êshra gazed at the book. "We have seen this before," she told Xalid in his language.

"Yan thinks it's important."

Ma'h'bri's head bobbed. He squinted. His bony finger crept across the page.

The watermark from the fish had caused a stain revealing symbols hidden in the texture. They looked to Yan like musical notations, a series of locating numbers one would find on a map and a final symbol, ONE, in the Common Tongue. As a child, Yan had used the juice of lemons on paper to write secret messages. The juice dried and disappeared; it could be read only when the paper was moved quickly back and forth over a candle's flame. The watermark from the fish had worked in much the same way to reveal the invisible ink.

Yan's heart now raced like a child's. The fish had made a discovery …

Ma'h'bri whispered, and H'Êshra leaned to look. She ran her finger across the page until it touched Ma'h'bri's.

The two fingers found the symbol: ONE.

Ma'h'bri stirred in Xalid's arms. He stood. H'Êshra and Ma'h'bri looked at each other. "This is what we have hoped for — the clue we have always sought. We must signal the *caeenri-beda* immediately!" they said. "Xalid! You must help us!"

"Of course!"

H'Êshra and Ma'h'bri spoke quickly, in five languages that Xalid understood. He nodded, then raced from the Font of Knowledge.

H'Êshra and Ma'h'bri looked at the fish, the living language. The fish swam triumphantly, spelling out good wishes and brave journey. H'Êshra and Ma'h'bri used a complicated sign language, thanking the fish for their invaluable help and insight.

Outside, the subtle winds increased. Dry leaves crackled through the air. Lightning pulsed like white snake tongues in the distant sky.

Xalid found Gyro and hurriedly explained what H'Êshra and Ma'h'bri needed. He pointed to a tower so tall it seemed lost in the troubled night sky.

"I'll get S'yen or Terra!" Gyro said.

"No!" Xalid countered. "They said it must be Lynai'seth!"

"Let's find her!"

The two Outcasts ran through the courtyard to the sleeping quarters of the children. Everyone was awake.

"Lynai'seth!" Gyro called. "We have a project."

"A project?"

"Bring your sword."

Lynai'seth nodded. She took up her sword and turned to the children. "All of you stay … here. Mind Terra."

"Yes," Terra said. "Mind me." She whispered to Lynai'seth, "There's no way they're going to mind me."

"Children," Lynai'seth commanded, "do as I say — or else!"

The children sat quietly. Ru'an bit her lips as if holding back a smile.

Lynai'seth followed Gyro into the night. "Do you smell trouble?" she asked as they headed for the turret.

"Shadow Beasts. And others — maybe Antibodies."

"How many?"

Gyro paused. "Like the stars."

Lynai'seth looked at him. "You joke."

"I wish I were."

"What do we do?"

"Xalid seems to think you and I can contact the *caeenri-beda*."

"What can two animals do against thousands?"

"Teach them a lesson." Gyro quickly explained to Lynai'seth what they needed to do according to Xalid's instructions.

Thick clouds filled the sky. Lightning struck in wicked daggers. Wind whistled through the trees.

Gyro and Lynai'seth hurried to the wooden door of a towering white building. Gyro swung open the door and charged inside. Lynai'seth followed.

They ran up a winding staircase. Wind swept through open windows. The passage howled in strident cries.

They ran in darkness. When lightning flashed, the tower and its stairs turned a stark, blinding white.

They continued running upwards in a spiral. At one point, Gyro crashed into a locked door. Lynai'seth came up behind him. She took the sword and jiggled the tip of it in the keyhole. The lock popped open.

"I'm impressed," Gyro said.

Lynai'seth smiled. "It's how I used to sneak out of my house."

They charged up the next spiral of steps, higher. The winds increased, the storms grew more violent, their flash and fury tearing open the dark skies. Rain fell, as sharp as needles.

Gyro and Lynai'seth struggled to reach the top of the tower. Gyro leaned into a door and shoved it open. They entered a small room. In the corner, on a pile of straw, lay the two objects they sought.

Lynai'seth grabbed the Locating Tripod, which was almost as tall as she was. Gyro took up the Horn, a spiralling device that looked like a golden cornucopia. The Horn was heavy; he had to hoist it in both arms.

They stepped through an open window, climbed twelve steps and stood atop a small platform. They were outside, the world raging around them, wind and storm slapping them like gnats. They quickly placed the Horn onto the Locating Tripod. Lynai'seth adjusted a small lens on the Tripod and squinted into it. "What am I looking for?" she shouted to Gyro.

"The direction Yan and Xalid found in a book," Gyro said. He repeated the numbers and coordinates Xalid had told him.

Lynai'seth's braided hair flailed about in the wind. "I don't see anything!"

"Keep looking!"

Lynai'seth blinked rainwater from her eyes and looked into the lens. "Wait — I see something! Turn the Horn!"

Gyro moved the Horn clockwise on the Locating Tripod.

"Too far! Move it back!"

Gyro rotated the Horn counter-clockwise.

He sniffed the air.

While Lynai'seth gazed through the lens, he looked down over the edge of the platform. The villa and Font of Knowledge looked like a mad quilt of darkness and light. The sleeping quarters were black and still. Trees bent sideways in the wind.

The main gate burst open.

Like volcanic lava, like flooding waters, like quicksand, thousands of Shadow Beasts poured into the villa.

"Oh ..." was all Gyro could say.

"What's wrong?" Lynai'seth cried.

"We've got guests."

Lynai'seth pulled away from the lens to look at him. She peered over the edge of the platform at the sea of Shadow Beasts forming below them.

"I've got to get back to the children!"

"First we use the Horn!"

Lynai'seth stared at Gyro. "Thank you for getting us this far. We almost reached HayVen."

"My pleasure," Gyro said with a nod and faint smile. He positioned himself next to the Horn to anchor it in the wind.

Lynai'seth wiped rain from her face. She stared intently into the lens. The device was a small metal cylinder, barely longer than her hand. She could see a disk of white inside the lens and two black crosshairs. As she slowly rotated the lens, she could see an occasional blink of light.

H'Êshra and Ma'h'bri had said she had the Sight, whatever that was. She had been able to see the white beast, the *caeenri-beda*, when no one else had. Lynai'seth concentrated. She tried to see without looking, to understand the violent night and where the creatures might be.

Suddenly, through the lens, she saw two white shapes.

"I found them!"

Gyro adjusted the Horn. Now it was up to him to follow Xalid's instructions and blow a signal for the *caeenri-beda*.

The Horn quivered in the wind. Lynai'seth wrapped her arms around it and held it in place. Gyro knelt by the small end of the Horn, drew a deep breath, and blew through it.

"*AHROOOO!*"

A fantastic, deep, bellowing note escaped the Horn, its sound pounding through the night. In this night of torment, when fierce wind battled with soft garden breezes, sound itself was in chaos. The bellowing Horn seemed to find its own path between the claps of thunder and howling wind.

Gyro blew a second note, a shorter third note. He paused. He blew five more notes. A final long note.

Nine notes from the Horn fought their way through deafening wind to reach the *caeenri-beda* and offer them direction.

Gyro waited to catch his breath.

The wind did not wait. It slapped Lynai'seth, and Gyro, and the Horn on its Locating Tripod. The legs of the Tripod buckled. The Horn crashed to the floor. It rolled. Gyro and Lynai'seth dove for it.

This time, the two Outcasts could not stop the Horn from falling off the platform. It fell like a thin stick into the swelling sea of Shadow Beasts.

Gyro leaned over the edge. It crumbled under his weight.

Before Lynai'seth could move a muscle, Gyro fell off the edge.

Chapter 29

The Shadow Beasts attacked the Font of Knowledge.

They moved with shattering power through the courtyards, fountains, gardens, dining hall and visiting chambers. They attacked with a strength beyond all human record, beyond all human imagining. They burst into the storage barns where the Outcasts had left their carts. The Shadow Beasts reduced the carts to splinters.

H'Êshra and Ma'h'bri closed the great doors of the Font before the first Shadow Beasts had attacked. They had sought the Outcasts but could not find any of them. Only Yan and Xalid remained within the Font. Only the fish and a few animals stood guard in this last museum marked for annihilation.

H'Êshra and Ma'h'bri winced as Shadow Beasts pounded against the door. They spoke to Yan. He understood. He grabbed the book containing the final clue. When the time came, he was to burn the book to ashes. Better to have the book fall to ash than fall into the wrong hands.

The three of them quickly gathered books, maps and critical museum pieces. H'Êshra and Ma'h'bri hurried down three flights of stairs, through a mirror, to a deep cell with a metal door as thick as the length of Yan's arm.

They hid precious artifacts and texts — remains of Dulunae.

The Shadow Beasts pounded relentlessly.

***

It seemed like ages ago.

When setting foot in the hallowed villa, the Outcasts had felt refreshed, their aches and pains gone, their wounds healed. Now, as trees buckled in the rainstorm, as fountains and statues fell and shattered on tiled floors, the healing world failed.

Pain had returned.

Terra felt the pain of all the Outcasts at one time. She doubled over, screaming. The repeated waves of pain crushed her.

Elsewhere, at the highest point of the villa, on a windswept platform, Lynai'seth leaned over the edge.

Gyro had fallen.

And had grabbed a window ledge whilst in mid-air.

He hung by his arms but could not get a foothold on the slick, rain-washed tower.

He was beyond Lynai'seth's reach. She ran from the platform to the winding staircase inside the tower.

Despite pounding wind and rain, despite the threatening sea of Shadow Beasts below, despite the brutal pull of the earth and loss of all hope, despite the return of their pain and illness, two Outcast boys found their one leader.

A sick, bony hand appeared over Gyro.

Oolo's hand. The one that a mother Shadow Beast had severed. That Terra had restored.

The hand reached for Gyro and held on tight. Tears welled in Oolo's eyes, but he refused to let his leader fall.

A pair of clumsy hands and arms held onto Oolo. Kg, who had known the joy of controlling his body for a time, now struggled to help Oolo pull Gyro into the small room in the tower.

Kg and Oolo strained to keep Gyro from falling. Kg felt his arms jerking, muscles twitching. Oolo was blind with pain.

Two boys, beaten into submission all their lives, found heroic fire within them.

They slowly pulled Gyro into the room.

He lunged to safety.

Oolo and Kg fell on the cold, wet floor. At that moment, Lynai'seth burst into the room.

The boys would never again be unknown heroes. While Gyro and Lynai'seth lived, they would sing the praises of Oolo and Kg.

"Thank you," Gyro gasped. "Thank you both for saving my life."

Oolo moaned, rubbing his hand. Kg rolled on the floor, his legs shaking. Lynai'seth leaned and held Kg. She gently lifted Oolo's hand and studied it.

"You're heroes," she said. She kissed Oolo's hand, kissed Kg's brow.

"Are the others in the tower?" Gyro asked.

Oolo nodded.

"Everyone safe?"

He nodded again.

Kg wanted to say, "Terra saved everyone," but all he could utter were moans and clicking sounds. He was back to normal, lost to the violent spasms that ruled his body and brain.

Gyro rose. "I've got to go."

Lynai'seth held Kg. "I'll stay here with the two of them for a while. Let us know what your lesson plan is."

Gyro smiled. "The lesson for today is surviving Shadow Beasts."

"That's a tough one."

Gyro returned to the winding staircase in the tower. As he descended, he discovered that Outcasts had hidden in nooks and crannies throughout the tower.

He found Tu'ghee T'an and Lhista T'an huddled in a dark corner in one of the lower levels of the tower. "Where's Ignis?" he asked them. The brother and sister said he had found a storeroom ten levels below that had made him happy.

Gyro smiled. "That's what I wanted to hear."

He ran down the staircase, calling to Outcasts at each level. He heard from Alamine and Amina, Klanga and Feelie, Mohir'a'qest and Zwyna, Ru'an and several other children.

"Whatever you do," Gyro warned, "don't go outside!"

"There are Shadow Beasts everywhere!" Zwyna cried.

"Everywhere!" Mohir'a'qest added.

"I'm going to find Ignis. Stay inside!"

Gyro thundered down the staircase. He stopped once to look out a window at the storm, at the swelling of Shadow Beasts below him. It looked as if the entire earth had come alive as a teeming mass of animal fur, claws, fangs and fiery red eyes. There were Shadow Beasts crawling on top of each other, snarling, fighting and biting.

He looked out another window in the direction he and Lynai'seth had chosen for aiming the Horn. No charging white creatures.

They didn't hear me, Gyro thought bitterly. *Or they can't get to us ...*

He kept running. He knew there was no escape for the Outcasts. Shadow Beasts surrounded them. This would be their final stand.

He wasn't about to die quietly, though. Gyro circled down the spiral staircase and cried out for Ignis.

Ignis sat in a room filled with crates. There was a foul odor, like sulphur. Other metallic smells. Gyro thought they were familiar but couldn't name them.

"Can you give us light?"

Ignis giggled.

"I take that as a yes."

Ignis giggled even louder. His fingers were fast at work, mixing powders in ceramic pots and glass vials. He stabbed long strings into the powdery concoctions. He told Gyro to leave the room with him. Ignis ran a number of strings from pots and vials on the window ledge, across the floor, under the door and out into the dim hallway. He gestured for Gyro to back away from the room.

"Light?" Gyro wondered.

Ignis laughed. In a snap, he created a tiny fire and lit the strings. The strings burned in bright yellow trails of flame, across the hallway, under the door, back into the room.

Alamine had been running down the staircase. He was panting for air. "Lynai'seth … she … she wanted you to know … she had a vision …"

"What vision?" Gyro asked.

"The … the white animals …"

"She saw them?"

"In the … beyond the … Shadow Beasts … but the white animals looked lost …"

Gyro turned sharply to Ignis. "We need light for the

white beasts!"

Ignis laughed, his ribs quivering.

Suddenly, there was an explosion. The closed door blew open. A choking cloud of smoke rolled over them. There was hissing, popping, more explosions, bursts of flame, a spray of sparks. Jets of glittering flame sprayed from the window up into the night sky. The jets burst into multi-colored fireworks that spread like golden spider webs across the sky. Plumes of red, yellow and blue exploded. White streaks lanced the raging winds and rain.

Pinwheels lifted and danced through the air.

All the while, Ignis laughed uncontrollably, living out his greatest dream: a firework display rivalling the shows chronicled in ancient times.

Gyro ran from level to level in the tower. He needed to find all the Outcasts and set up a line of communication among them. He had one girl or boy in each part of the tower learn a series of Common Tongue words and hand signals to help alert others. Gyro didn't want to risk having everyone cornered in one room at the moment, but he also didn't want anyone isolated and trapped.

He determined that the tower would become their final fortress against the Shadow Beasts.

The fireworks continued, bathing the tower and surrounding villa in colorful light.

Some of the Shadow Beasts tried running away as sparks showered upon them.

Gyro found Terra on the bottom floor in the tower. The sleeves of her shirt were torn, spotted with blood. S'yen sat next to her. His Battle Gloves were caked with fur and blood.

"Are you all right?" Gyro asked.

Terra smiled weakly. "Getting better. Healer, heal thyself, as they say."

"What happened?"

"We're not happy and healthy here anymore. The pains have come back. I felt everybody's pain at the same time. Meanwhile, S'yen and I found a few Shadow Beasts trying to get through the tower doors here. A big fight. We won. I used up the last of my sleeping gases."

Gyro leaned. He gently stroked her hair and kissed her forehead.

Terra smiled. "Does this mean we're engaged?"

"I should be so lucky."

Terra shifted. Her shoulder was bleeding. "Tell me something — is this our last battle?"

"Not if I can help it."

"Are there fireworks outside? I keep seeing flashing lights."

"Ignis is putting on a show."

"I thought I was dying."

"Not on my watch, you don't."

Terra touched Gyro's arm. "You'll make a great teacher someday."

"You're a great healer right now. Rest." Gyro gestured for S'yen to keep watch over Terra. S'yen nodded.

Gyro crossed the room. Shadow Beasts pounded against the door. Their snarling and howling became a single, deafening voice of destruction. Wind and rain slashed the sky. Fireworks keened and wheeled in the air.

Gyro didn't say anything to S'yen or Terra. He could smell rain, the electric charge of lightning, the metallic drift of the fireworks, wet fur, smoke, fire — and blood.

It was the same smells he had encountered repeatedly in communities ravaged by Antibodies.

The smell of death.

If these were to be his last moments in this life, they would be his best. He had done the impossible and had brought together forty-three other Outcasts — forty-four with that monster, Dav'yn — and had led them across the world to this Font of Knowledge, to a place closely resembling HayVen.

The children had known happiness. The absence of pain and fear. Kg had spoken a word.

Everyone had laughed again.

Except Jax and Marina …

Are they alive? Will I see —

Somehow, a Shadow Beast had climbed up and jumped through an open window in the room. Two.

Gyro stepped backwards towards Terra and S'yen. S'yen was already on his feet, Battle Gloves on his hands. Terra struggled to her feet.

The three of them moved to the middle of the room. They stood back-to-back.

Fireworks burst, casting the chamber in bright green light.

The blood-red eyes of the Shadow Beasts gazed at the three humans in the center of the room.

***

Lynai'seth was still high in the tower. She leaned out a

window. Rain spattered her face. Bolts of lightning dug through darkness.

The last of the fireworks rose, burst in the sky, then settled, falling like bright dust into nothingness.

Shadow Beasts ran below, coursing throughout the villa with the fury of a flood.

The end had begun.

She hated feeling helpless. It was not right for a member of the Shi'vaal Community to stand passively as the world fell to ruin.

Gyro had worked wonders so far. The Outcasts had all come too far to end like this.

She looked over her shoulder at Oolo and Kg, who were seated in a corner of the room, in quiet darkness.

She turned back and squinted into the night. Lightning struck the distant hills.

Something emerged from the burst of lightning. It glowed like white flame.

A tree —

No. It's moving.

Lynai'seth watched as the ball of pure white light moved in and out of shadows. It drew closer to the tower, moving at an incredible speed.

The ball of light seemed to split in half and move in opposite directions.

Lynai'seth stared. Then she knew.

One of the *caeenri-beda* was approaching.

It moved with the power and authority of lightning, as if nothing on earth could stand in its way.

The Horn had worked. She and Gyro had summoned the white beast.

She feared that the Shadow Beasts would devour the *caeenri-beda*. It was one small creature against thousands.

Lynai'seth felt her breath catch. She looked below and saw a Shadow Beast leap through a window on the ground level. Two of them. Three. Word had gotten to her through the chain of communication in the tower that Terra, S'yen and Gyro were on the ground level.

She had to go down and help.

"Wait here! I'll be back!" she told Kg and Oolo. Lynai'seth grabbed her sword and ran down the spiral staircase.

Other Outcasts saw her. They already knew that Shadow Beasts had climbed through the tower windows.

"What do we do?" Mohir'a'qest asked.

Alamine patted his arm. "We fight to the last breath."

Lynai'seth smiled. "You're all so brave. I am honored to know you."

"Go get the Shadow Beasts!" Zwyna cried.

Lynai'seth left the room.

She moved quickly down the steps to the ground level. She stood in the passageway. She could hear the growling of the three Shadow Beasts in the next room.

She held up her sword. Listened. Waited.

She thought she heard Terra's voice.

"Don't do anything," Terra was saying from inside the room. "They won't hurt us."

"Why?" Gyro hissed.

"They're good."

"How can you tell?"

"Look at the marking between their eyes."

"They all have diamond shapes. I've never seen those shapes before."

"I know about markings on the forehead. The diamonds appear when the Shadow Beasts are about to help us. These are the same Beasts who helped us fight the Antibodies."

Gyro paused. "You sure?"

"Almost positive."

"Almost?"

Lynai'seth tightened her grip on the handle of her sword. She would count to three, then attack.

One.

Outside, Shadow Beasts pounded without mercy against the doors of the tower.

Two.

A howling cry filled the air, louder than thunder, louder than the growling of the Shadow Beasts. Lynai'seth thought she saw a flash of white light between the cracks of the tower wall where she stood.

Probably more fireworks. Or lightning.

She listened. Terra was silent.

She leaned enough to see Gyro, Terra and S'yen standing in the middle of the room, the three Shadow Beasts surrounding them.

Three —

Lynai'seth swung the sword over her head. She was about to leap into the room and lash out at the Shadow Beasts. A single streak of pure white light across a wall stopped her.

There was rumbling outside, but the pounding against the tower door had stopped.

The shrieking grew louder. Lynai'seth lowered her sword.

There was shuffling and crashing, as if the Shadow Beasts were fighting to gain supremacy within their own pack.

The shrieking was fevered, ear-shattering. Lynai'seth winced. Light poured through windows, cracks, holes and nooks, as if the tower were not a solid fortress but a casual arrangement of loose, ill-fitting stones.

Lynai'seth stumbled into the room. Gyro, Terra and S'yen were also covering their ears. The Shadow Beasts looked at her, then jumped. Their muscled, furry bodies moved with startling grace.

They jumped out the windows and joined the pack outside.

Gyro pointed to the ceiling. "UP!" he shouted.

He grabbed Terra's hand, who in turn held S'yen's shoulder. S'yen slipped off one of his Battle Gloves and reached for Lynai'seth.

The four Outcasts climbed up the staircase to higher ground.

They rose several levels, then leaned out a pair of windows to see what was happening below them.

The Outcasts had fought Antibodies. They had seen the Seven Statues in the desert. They had battled Shadow Beasts. They had seen crystal caves and amber canyons. They had ridden G'unk-g'unks.

Nothing prepared them for what they now saw:

The *caeenri-beda* was leading the Shadow Beasts. It glowed white as lightning and ran outside the walls of the villa and

Font of Knowledge.

Hundreds, thousands of Shadow Beasts followed.

The *caeenri-beda* ran in a wide circle around the villa.

A second time.

A third.

Instead of slowing or running off into the night, the *caeenri-beda* ran faster. The Shadow Beasts also pounded along the earth in quick pursuit.

The Beasts ran faster and faster, around and around the Font.

The rainstorm stopped.

Clouds parted.

A column of dust, wind and white light rose from the circling Shadow Beasts. The thousands seemed to become a single blur.

The thousands created a sound beyond the thundering of dark skies or cracking of shifting earth, beyond the burst of volcanoes or voice of an avalanche.

The *caeenri-beda* and Shadow Beasts were panting, snarling, pounding the earth, clawing the rock and debris, tearing a wide circular path around the villa as if this was their sole reason for staying alive.

By now, most of the Outcasts were looking out windows in various parts of the tower. No one could speak.

Finally, Lynai'seth was able to give voice to the one question on all their minds:

"What does it mean?"

Chapter 30

E verything is a blur ...
Jax wasn't sure where he had been or where he was
going. All he knew was that, at the moment, he and Marina
were riding on the backs of two white beasts.

The beasts seemed to be able to change their shapes at will,
larger, smaller, wider, leaner. They were more powerful than
Shadow Beasts. They looked to Jax like pets the Antibodies
might have had around their homes. If such monsters lived
in homes.

Jax tried organizing in his mind what had happened since
he had found Lynai'seth's second hair band on the plateau. He
had held it side-by-side with the first. The two bands formed
a scene of a ravine and a river. Along the river were five trees.
Two white objects — maybe boulders or animals — sat at the
foot of the middle tree.

Jax and Marina had waited on the plateau for the Shadow
Beasts to run off. By dawn, the fierce animals had disappeared.
Marina and Jax quickly climbed down the side of the plateau
and headed southwest.

By now, there was no doubt between them, no confusion.
Only resolve. They had to find the Outcasts. They hadn't come
this far only to fail.

Jax knew that Marina was holding back her running pace
for his sake. He had eaten the underground plants and felt
strong again, but there was no way he could keep up with
Marina's breakneck speed.

Then, after a time, we found the river, Jax thought as his white beast jumped over a boulder. He had taken Marina's advice and had studied the language of the verdant new setting. Trees, bushes, rocks, grass, water, mud all had stories to tell — about how old they were, about who or what had been there to help or hurt them. Listen to them, Marina had said, and their language would tell grand histories.

Lynai'seth had carefully thought out the placement of her hair bands — first in the crystal caves, then on the plateau. If there were a third one here, the placement would be critical.

Jax looked. The trees seemed randomly scattered. Lynai'seth's Shi'vaal clothing suggested, though, that there were patterns beneath the apparent chaos.

In the distance, in emerald light, sat two large white rocks at the foot of a tree. The tall tree was the third of five that stretched their limbs proudly skyward.

In a chink of the rock, a familiar object.

The third hair band.

As Jax touched the hair band, two gigantic white beasts appeared. Marina grabbed her quarterstaff; Jax stood ready to fight.

The animals stretched their two front legs and leaned, as if bowing to them.

"What are they doing?" Jax whispered.

Marina studied the animals, then smiled. "Offering us a ride."

"Are you sure?"

"If they had wanted to attack us, we wouldn't be having this conversation."

"You *trust* these creatures?"

Marina looked at him. "I'm surprised, Jax. Usually you're the one who trusts everything."

Jax grimaced. "I've grown cautious in my old age."

Marina lowered her quarterstaff, slowly approached one of the white beasts and carefully climbed on its back, holding its fur with her free hand. The animal made a gentle sound, indicating acceptance.

"Come on," Marina urged.

Jax crept towards the second beast. "Easy, boy. Easy. Easy, boy."

"How do you know it's a boy?" Marina wondered.

"Easy … girl. Boy. Whichever you are. Please don't bite or kill me."

Jax slipped onto the back of the second beast. He looped his fingers through the animal's thick fur and held on tightly.

"Now what do we —"

Before Jax could finish his question, the two white beasts reared backwards, pounced and ran with breathtaking speed along the river. They leapt over high rocks, slammed their way through thick brush and kicked up clouds of dirt as they charged into the unknown.

And here we are now, Jax thought, *riding in a rainstorm to who knows where …*

The white beasts paused. They had been running faster and longer than any human ever could. Amazingly, they were not panting for breath. They stood as if simply resting on a calm afternoon.

"Jax!" Marina cried. "Listen!"

Jax heard a deep, mournful cry in the night. Another. Nine notes from a distant instrument. He felt the white beast stirring. It raised its thick neck and looked at the other beast. They muttered something to each other.

"What is it?" Jax called to Marina. "A warning?"

"I think so!"

"What do we do?"

Before she could answer, the white beasts began running again. Dry channels of dirt were now overflowing with rainwater. Ancient trees fell in the wind, their roots looking like desperate fingers pleading for help.

Lightning dug into the hills to the left and right of them. The white beasts kept running.

Ahead, the sky burst into a multitude of colored lights.

"Fireworks!" Marina cried. During festivals in her Quae Community, voyagers from distant lands on Dulunae thrilled people with their spectacular fireworks displays. The one they saw now rivalled the best shows in her community.

She had a thought — only for the tiniest moment — she was to see a Festival of Lights with the one betrothed to her.

Jax …

She released the thought. The hope.

The white beasts clawed their way through mudslides running down rocky walls.

Suddenly, they both slammed to a halt.

Jax and Marina didn't.

Marina tumbled off the side of the animal and fell in a patch of muddy grass.

Jax flew forward, landing face-first in a bush.

Before they knew what was happening, one of the white beasts ran off in the direction of the fireworks.

The second beast leaned, allowing them to climb on top of it. Its fur was matted flat from the rain.

Marina stood, wiping mud from her legs. She climbed on the white beast. She looked at Jax. "What are you waiting for?"

Jax worked his way from the bush. He pulled leaves from his mouth. "Well, there's no place for me to sit."

"Sit right behind me!"

"Maybe I'll wait for the next ride."

"Jax!"

Jax reluctantly climbed onto the white beast. It seemed to expand its length to accommodate him.

"Put your arms around me!" Marina said.

Jax hesitated. "You won't hit me again, will you?"

Marina looked over her shoulder at him. She was smiling.

Jax did something he never thought imaginable in his lifetime. He held Marina. As he locked his arms around her, she squeezed his forearm with her free hand, as if to reassure him. Her long black hair was wet and hung down thick as a curtain. Jax was close enough to smell the pure ocean breeze of her hair. Oddly enough, it felt like —

Home.

As they got comfortable on the white beast, lightning flashed — blinding them — and thunder rolled. The beast jumped through the maze of rocks, away from the sound of the Horn, away from the fireworks, away from any signs of safety.

Into darkness.

Jax smelled something foul — like decaying food burning

in heaps. The land and surrounding walls of rock were black and oily. Even the white beast, as nimble as it was, had trouble keeping its balance on some of the slick plates of rock they crossed. The animal slowed its pace.

"Where do you think it's taking us?" Jax asked.

"I don't know, Jax. I can't understand the language of this place."

The white beast walked up a greasy incline.

"Marina," Jax said, "are we going to die tonight?"

She paused. "We might."

"Then you need to know something."

"What, Jax?"

"You know where HayVen is? Right here. With you."

Marina leaned and looked back at him. He couldn't tell if it was rainwater or tears streaking her cheek.

The white beast stopped. Its massive head rolled back and forth, as if it were listening for something mere humans would never hear.

It reared back.

Too late.

Something as black as oil, as powerful as rock, fell from the sky and hit the white beast. The animal fell. Jax tumbled backwards. Marina crashed onto her shoulder, her quarterstaff spinning off along the ground into darkness.

Another thing dropped from the oily night. Three. Four. Five.

The white beast was fighting with one of the predators.

Jax crawled to Marina's side. "You all right?"

"Yes!" Marina cried. She rolled to a crouching position.

"What have we got?"

"Five!" Jax cried. As his eyes adjusted, they widened with horror. "No —"

"*Een-Yesssh,*" one of the creatures said.

Jax opened his mouth but couldn't speak.

"Jax!" Marina said.

"*Een-Jaahs,*" the creature mocked.

Jax felt as if he had swallowed the surrounding oil.

The creatures stood as tall as humans. They had antennae that coiled in long whips, narrow heads, thick bodies, furry arms and pincers for hands.

And they had almost human faces.

Faces that Jax recognized.

He finally found his voice. "It's — *Dav'yn!*"

"*Een-DaaVenn,*" the creature taunted.

It was Dav'yn with three other Outcasts, Kon-gor, S'h'ta and Cobin-4. Bayne fought with the white beast.

"*Naa-DaaVenn,*" the Dav'yn creature said.

"*Een-*CHITIN!*"

"Chitin?" Marina said.

"*Een-MaREEna. Een-*CHITIN!*"

Somehow, Dav'yn and the others had transformed themselves into hideous insect creatures. Dav'yn swung a pincer, slicing Jax's shirt.

Marina rolled and grabbed her quarterstaff. She tried hitting Kon-gor as hard as she could. He tilted backwards but regained his balance. His mouth twisted into a sick smile.

"*Een! Een!*"

"*Een!*" the other creatures cried, mocking Marina.

Her most powerful blow had had no effect on Kon-gor. His skin was as strong as stone. He looked like a towering dung beetle on hind legs, pincers snapping in the air.

Bayne was strangling the white beast. The animal swung its neck, flinging him against a wall of rock. Bayne fell, rolled, then stood unharmed.

"Jax!" Marina cried.

"*Een-Jaahs, Een-Jaahs,*" Dav'yn taunted.

"We can't hurt them!"

Dav'yn's head looked crushed and narrow. His large black eyes sat on either side of his face. He grinned, revealing a row of sharp orange fangs. Somehow, he was able to speak in the Common Tongue — but in a way that sounded as if he were underwater.

"*Een-yew* cannot hurt CHITIN, but CHITIN will — kill *een-yew!*"

"Dav'yn!" Marina said. "Listen to me! We need to find the Outcasts! There are Shadow Beasts everywhere!"

Dav'yn recoiled. "*Een! Een-BEEST!* Kill *een-BEEST!*"

"Leave us alone!"

Dav'yn swung an arm, but Marina defended herself with a quick sweep of her quarterstaff. Cobin-4 lunged at her, but she twisted sideways to avoid him. Cobin-4 crashed into a boulder. He simply shook his head, and laughed.

Jax watched S'h'ta. He could see S'h'ta clearly, even in darkness. The creature's antennae snapped in the air and coiled around Jax's arm. Before S'h'ta could attack, Jax pulled with all his might, sending S'h'ta into the charred base of an ancient, dead tree.

Jax studied the creatures for any signs of vulnerability. There were none. Dav'yn and the others had become Chitin, creatures without identity whose purpose was to serve and destroy.

Jax saw that they were truly like insects — they jumped about, crawled, slid, fell and rose again. They seemed incapable of coordinating an attack.

He whistled to Marina, and she returned the signal.

Marina charged at Dav'yn with her quarterstaff. He swung pincers and antennae. At the last moment, she stabbed the quarterstaff into the ground and vaulted over him, kicking Cobin-4 and S'h'ta. They fell on their backs.

Jax crouched and swung his leg, knocking Dav'yn to the ground.

The white beast grabbed Bayne in its jaws and swung him into Kon-gor.

All five Chitin lay on the ground.

For a moment.

They jumped up and laughed. "*Een! Een!*"

They snapped their antennae, swung claws, crawled, bounced, writhed. Kon-gor slammed an arm into Jax's stomach, knocking the wind from him. The creature clamped its pincers on Marina's quarterstaff but recoiled in pain as soon as it touched it. She poked the staff in its eye, sending Kon-gor backwards.

Jax was on all fours, gasping for air. He smelled something familiar — something used to repair rooftops in his Kerta Community.

Dav'yn stood over him and pounded Jax on the back of his neck.

"*Een-Jaahs.* Die."

Dav'yn struck again.

Jax refused to fall.

Dav'yn hit him a third time.

Instead of giving in to pain, Jax grew livid with anger. He would not be beaten again. He would not let anyone harm Marina.

"Eeeyah!"

The wild cry came from Jax this time, not Dav'yn. Jax pounced on Dav'yn, knocking him to the ground. They wrestled, Jax struggled to keep Dav'yn's sharp pincers from stabbing him.

The white beast jumped into Kon-gor, Cobin-4 and Bayne. Marina swung a fist into S'h'ta's eye, sending the creature reeling down an oily slope.

"*Een-haayte-yew,*" Dav'yn said, a green substance dribbling from his lips. He repeatedly tried slashing Jax with his pincers.

"I'm not so thrilled about you!" Jax said. "You're uglier than ever … and you stink!"

"*EEEEEEN!*"

Kon-gor, Cobin-4 and Bayne stood again and jumped on the white beast. S'h'ta clawed his way up the slope and attacked Marina again.

Jax was able to kick Dav'yn away, but Dav'yn rolled and swung his razor arms through the air.

"Jax!" Marina called. "We can't stop them! We need a plan!"

Jax kicked Dav'yn off him again. "I have one! Get the Chitin to follow me!"

Jax scrambled to his feet. He ran towards a familiar smell. Deep in the black rock, chasms opened, the maw of the underworld widened. The chasms and ravines emitted a smell of tar, the same substance Jax's father used to fix their rooftop after a windstorm.

Jax watched carefully as he darted through the pockmarks, holes, cracks and crevasses in the earth. His eyes saw this black maze as if he were running in broad daylight.

Marina followed his trail. The white beast was bleeding

but still able to run after them.

The five Chitin seemed to leap, float through the air and drop before them.

Jax dodged.

Dav'yn almost slashed him, but Marina was able to knock him off his feet with her quarterstaff. The white beast jumped on Dav'yn's chest, crushing air from his lungs.

Still, Dav'yn rose.

Jax moved as he never had before, with skill, agility and confidence. He had learned from Marina. He would not let her down, ever again.

Dav'yn's antennae curled around his throat, tightening. Jax gasped, trying to pry the antennae off him.

"*Een-die ...*"

Marina and the white beast were too busy fighting the others to help. Jax choked.

His left foot stopped on the edge of a deep pit. His right foot hovered over thin air. The earth exhaled the smell of tar.

Jax glanced down the chasm only once. He grabbed the antennae and jumped.

He and Dav'yn plunged into the abyss. Jax landed on a small ledge he had spotted.

Dav'yn did not.

Jax braced himself for the final tug. Dav'yn slammed against the chasm wall, releasing the antennae before they could drag Jax down into the black recesses of rock.

Dav'yn fell.

The white beast seemed momentarily revived. It carried Kongor, Cobin-4 and Bayne on its back. The Chitin swung their deadly arms and encircled the white beast with their antennae, but the animal fought back. It jumped over crags of rock, slammed into a wall and ran towards the edge of the pit.

At the last moment, the white beast jammed to a halt. The three Chitin flew off the white beast, plunging into the chasm. They dropped within Jax's reach and kept falling.

Marina was waiting for S'h'ta to charge her. She grabbed his arms, fell on her back and flipped him into the pit with the others.

Marina looked over the edge. "Jax! You all right?"

"Yes! I'm coming up!"

"What about the Chitin?"

"They're in a sticky situation."

Marina extended her quarterstaff to Jax. "Get up here!"

Jax managed to climb from the pit. He stood with Marina and the white beast at the edge.

"Jax," Marina said, "they are — were — our friends."

"Speak for yourself. I never liked Dav'yn. Now I *really* don't like him."

"What happened to them?"

"Well, they turned into big bugs. Oolo would like them."

"Are they dead?"

"No. The pit isn't too deep. At least, I don't think it is. But it's filled with enough sticky tar to hold them for a while. Listen."

They heard the cry of the Chitin echoing deep in the pit: "*Een! Een! Een!*"

Jax shook his head. "They don't sound too happy."

"We have to get out of here."

They turned to the white beast. The animal looked mangled, its thick white fur now bloodied, shredded and matted with mud. Still, the white beast bowed for them. Marina and Jax climbed onto its back.

The white beast didn't move as quickly as it had. It walked slowly and deliberately through the foul fields of oil and tar.

Somewhere, the underworld trembled as if with deep displeasure.

Rocks tumbled from high cliffs.

Then all grew silent.

Two Outcasts rode on the back of the white beast to a new world.

"Jax," Marina said, "I'm glad you're all right."

"Marina, I'm glad you are, too. I can't do this without you."

"Be careful. Those are serious words where I come from."

"I am being serious."

Marina paused. "Do you have any idea where we're going?"

"No. But there must be a reason for all this."

The white beast climbed a hill. The surrounding land might have been vital and alive, once. There were tree stumps, river beds, weeds, vines and a random scatter of wildflowers that lived despite the grim nature of the black soil.

They saw rundown shacks of wood and mud that had collapsed, worn by innumerable storms. The shacks sat like tombstones honoring a time and people long lost to the shifting winds of Dulunae.

The land was barren and broken. The white beast trudged over a small wooden bridge that groaned from their weight.

They crossed the bridge. The white beast walked across a sad piece of earth, cracked and charred.

Marina tilted her head. "Jax," she whispered. "I hear something."

"Chitin?"

"No. Something low and soft."

"Where?"

The white beast stopped. Marina slid off the animal. She placed her quarterstaff on the ground and held out her hand to Jax. "Come with me."

Jax jumped at the chance to hold Marina's hand.

They walked together, slowly, carefully, to a sound only Marina could hear.

They walked together to a place in the night only Jax could see.

They walked as a couple.

The white beast watched.

It seemed as if this foul, fetid land gasped for air like an ancient creature suddenly seeking life.

The land held its breath, waiting.

A new language of the land was forming. It was a simple, clean, direct language. If it could be translated into the Common Tongue, it would be a single word: *Hope.*

Marina and Jax walked forward. It might have been a trick of light in the night, or something more —

They saw an "angle of rainbow" along an old rock wall.

The same "angle of rainbow" Yan had spoken about, in another time and place.

Marina and Jax followed the rainbow. The white beast kept to the shadows.

Marina listened. Jax looked. Together they saw something.

Something impossible in this land of the dead, something magnificent to behold.

Chapter 31

Elsewhere, Antibodies poured from holes in the earth, caves, burrows, any dark, dank shadow, and marched towards the Font of Knowledge. They crushed anything blocking their way. They destroyed all living creatures trapped in their path.

They were as powerful as storms, fires, earthquakes and volcanoes.

They were thousands of creatures moving with one purpose.

If the planet Dulunae were itself a living creature, its rivers would have seemed like endless tears, flowing mournfully as the disease of Antibodies spread.

***

At first, the Outcasts in the tower thought the Shadow Beasts were exciting. The animals were running in a circular path around them, faster with each passing moment.

Then, they grew frightened. The sky was deep green, like bile. Trees fell. Rocks showered down on the tower from the force of the Shadow Beasts. Their yelping and howling became a single, strident cry.

As the night wore on, the Outcasts grew tired and angry. There was a limited supply of food and water in the tower, and they had already run out of bread.

"Make them stop!" the children screamed.

The *caeenri-beda* and Shadow Beasts did not stop.

At dawn, the earth shook. The tower trembled.

Gyro stood at a window in the highest level of the tower. He froze. He smelled something in the air. He saw the unmistakable flow of Antibodies headed downhill, towards them.

His heart sank and seemed to turn to dust. He had run out of ideas.

Gyro looked to Lynai'seth, Terra, S'yen, anyone, for answers.

There were none.

He wondered what H'Êshra and Ma'h'bri could tell him.

***

In the Font of Knowledge, H'Êshra and Ma'h'bri learned about something new, something as primitive as the human race itself.

Fear.

They were old and tired. They had struggled against a world gone mad, a world where wisdom, knowledge, kindness and hope crumbled to the wilder forces. All the things they had collected in this Font of Knowledge — the books, paintings, sculptures, artifacts, tapestries, garments, suits of armor, weaponry, tools — seemed just that: *things.* Not symbols of human perfection but tired toys, best forgotten.

They peered out the window at the circling of the Shadow Beasts. Their friend, guardian, companion, the *caeenri-beda,* could only keep them running for so long before the final attack began.

The other *caeenri-beda* was lost in the night.

They spoke to each other in a thousand languages, each language bearing their message of sadness, loss and despair.

They were saying goodbye to each other.

Their words echoed through the empty halls and corridors in the Font of Knowledge. Their sad parting lifted like doves on a final flight into the unknown.

The Font of Knowledge shivered like a human spine, chilled.

***

Xalid walked through the Font of Knowledge, seeing for the first and last time a magnificent structure dedicated to art, intellect, history, culture, diversity and joy. To him, the Knowers had been the stuff of legends, a people of fantasy, unknown and untouchable.

Until now.

He could hear the echoing voices of H'Êshra and Ma'h'bri and understood some of what they were saying.

Farewell …

He had seen his own community die, heard his own family cry farewell, so he knew the end was near.

He felt no fear. Only resignation. He decided to spend his last moments in this grand and glorious harbor dedicated to all that was good and interesting on this troubled planet.

A wall cracked near him.

***

The cracking of a wall in the Font of Knowledge startled Yan, bringing him from his dreams and visions back to the *here and now.* He hated the *here and now,* the brute reality of Dulunae. Better to imagine how things might be rather than keep staring at how they really are.

The *here and now* was full of howling, like mad demons screeching from deep catacombs and ancient ruins, free to plague the world. The *here and now* was full of Shadow Beasts, and that strange white beast, running around the villa and crying wildly.

If only he could make them stop.

Yan's family had convinced him that he could do anything, as long as he cooperated with the community. He had no community now, only these strange boys and girls who roamed the harsh landscapes of Dulunae in search of HayVen.

The cries outside grew louder. Deafening. Maddening. It was like hearing his sick little brother screaming all night, on and on, for ages. Like hearing his sister play the *zyk'ded,* a pointless stringed instrument that could have been put to better use as an instrument of torture.

The *here and now* was full of languages, gibbering, wild sounds, endless noise.

In his community, Yan had run to a secret cave in times of grief. He listened to the sweet music of silence, flat, serene, peaceful. He often wondered how he might impose this silence on the screaming, screeching world.

His only answer was music.

He had constructed something he called a *yn'swyn,* a curling ceramic instrument similar to winding staircases in this Font of Knowledge. He poured water down the *yn'swyn* and rotated thin strips of gold in the flow. The water trickled, then rose again through a series of tiny pulleys. The notes could be high-pitched, like those of birds, or low, like the growling of lions.

Music.

There was no way to make music here, to stop the attack of the Shadow Beasts, to bring order to the *here and now.*

A wall cracked even wider. Water gushed from the crack, like his *yn'swyn*.

And then he knew.

He thought of what had happened in the desert, at the feet of the Seven Statues. He thought of what H'Êshra and Ma'h'bri had taught him.

He knew!

He ran past H'Êshra and Ma'h'bri to the door of the Font of Knowledge. Before they could react, he swung it open, closed it behind him and ran out into the world of maddening screams.

***

The Antibodies heard the animal screams. They saw the villa, the Font of Knowledge. They would spend little time destroying it. The ground would soon be level and forgotten. Their black hearts pumped madly in their transparent chests. Their lungs inflated, deflated as they breathed foul air. Their muscles tightened and relaxed, tightened and shifted as they ran faster. Their bones lifted, fell, twisted in a symphony of madness.

***

The *caeenri-beda* leading the race of Shadow Beasts around the villa could smell the approaching Antibodies. It had understood the message of the Horn, had seen the magic of fireworks in the night sky, and had used the opportunity to lead the Shadow Beasts on a desperate attack.

The *caeenri-beda* was a leader, but it needed a mission, a plan.

***

"The plan is to get the Horn," Gyro told the Outcasts. They were sitting in a tower room five levels from the ground.

"Are you crazy?" Terra cried.

"Yes."

"And you believe Yan?"

"Yes."

Yan sat trembling in a corner of the room. It had been harrowing running in the *here and now* from the Font of Knowledge to the tower.

"Didn't the Horn fall off the top of the tower?" Terra asked.

"I'm looking for volunteers," Gyro told everyone. "You can stay here in the tower or go outside and help us with the Horn."

"The Shadow Beasts will get us!" a boy cried.

"The Beasts!"

"Beasts!"

"Make them stop!"

"Even if they do stop," Terra said, "there are …" her voice trailed off.

"Antibodies," Gyro said.

Some of the children began crying again. "Ant-bodies? More than ten?"

Gyro nodded sadly. "More than ten."

"I'm staying!"

"Not going!"

"No!"

"It's all right," Gyro said. "You can stay here. We'll be right back."

The children looked at each other. Oolo stood. He helped Kg to his feet. He smiled at Gyro and nodded.

S'yen rose. Ru'an stood next to him.

Lynai'seth ran into the room. She had been looking for the Horn from a higher level in the tower. "I saw the Horn!" she said, out of breath. "It's still in one piece!"

"There's one good bit of news," Terra said.

"Those of you who are coming with us need to hold each other's hands. Tightly!" Gyro told the Outcasts. "The Shadow Beasts are making a terrible storm. It's extremely dangerous. If it gets too bad for you outside, run back in here."

He looked at them. He was asking children to step out into a wild windstorm while Shadow Beasts circled them and Antibodies raced from the hilltops.

"This is some field trip you're taking us on," Terra said. "What's next — jumping into an active volcano?"

Gyro smiled. "That's for extra credit."

He led the Outcasts downstairs to the main doorway. He pried open the door. Dust, leaves, twigs and animal fur blew in their faces. Gyro held Lynai'seth's hand. She, in turn, held Yan's hand. He held Terra. Terra grabbed S'yen.

The Outcasts formed a chain as they crept into the storm.

In the end, no one stayed behind in the tower. Klanga was the last to leave. She held Feelie tightly with her free hand.

Gyro thought he saw the *caeenri-beda* slow its pace to look at him. Then the mad dash of Shadow Beasts continued.

Gyro led the Outcasts along white cement walls. They slid like shadows.

Lynai'seth pointed directions.

The Horn lay in the middle of a courtyard in a pile of debris, under the large arching arm of an old tree limb. Its side was dented, but the instrument was intact.

There was a gasp, a slowing of wind. Gyro used the moment to rush to the middle of the courtyard.

The others formed a circle around him.

Xalid had been watching from a window in the Font of Knowledge. He ran from the building to join his friends. H'Êshra and Ma'h'bri were nowhere to be found.

They were Outcasts. Orphans. Those left behind by Antibodies. The last of their communities. The scraps from a banquet.

They fought with each other. They didn't understand each other. Sometimes they hated each other.

Now they stood together in a final circle of strength and resolve.

The Outcasts dug through the debris. They clawed their way. The green winds swirled. The Shadow Beasts cried with abandon.

Finally, Gyro grabbed the Horn. He yanked it from under the tree branch. Lynai'seth helped him prop it on top of a pile of wood. They aimed the mouth of the Horn towards the main gate of the villa.

Beyond the villa, the Shadow Beasts ran.

Beyond the Shadow Beasts, the Antibodies charged, their towering bodies a mass of muscle and sinew.

Yan had told Gyro he needed seven Outcasts to use the Horn. Gyro would be the first, then Terra, Ru'an, Alamine, Amina, Lynai'seth and, finally, Yan.

The first of the Antibodies reached the ravine. They dove into the pack of racing Shadow Beasts. The Beasts struck back at them.

The final battle had begun.

The Outcasts tightened the circle around the seven. Dust blinded them. Rocks struck their faces and chests. Twigs stung like darts.

Gyro took a deep breath and blew through the Horn.

The note sounded but seemed weak and pointless against the tide of Shadow Beasts.

Terra blew the Horn. Ru'an stiffened her tiny body and blew through the Horn with all her might. Nothing happened. She tried again. A tiny note sounded.

Alamine shut his eyes and blew a strange, hissing sound. He tried again. Amina blew her note on the Horn, then gasped for air and started coughing. Lynai'seth easily sounded her note, which was loud, melodic, piercing. Gyro thought he saw the *caeenri-beda* turn its head to listen to her.

Finally, Yan blew a note on the Horn.

The sky was deep green, the wind was brutal. The Shadow Beasts kept running.

Antibodies began seeping through the ring of Shadow Beasts encircling the villa.

The Outcasts drew closer to Gyro and the six others by the Horn. The winds whipped furiously. Sticks and rocks pummelled them. The Outcasts would defend Gyro and the other six to the end.

Gyro wanted to try the Horn again. He organized everyone in single file and had them blow the Horn in rapid succession.

The seven of them began to play something more than single notes.

They tried a third time. A fourth.

Before they tried for a fifth time, Gyro saw the first Antibody weaving its way downhill, through the Shadow Beasts, towards the entrance of the villa. Gyro cringed. It was too late to shuffle everyone back into the tower.

They played the Horn again.

This time, the *caeenri-beda* slowed its pace and looked directly into Gyro's eyes as it passed by him.

The *caeenri-beda* finally had its mission, its plan.

The Outcasts played the Horn a sixth time.

The seventh time, someone — some*thing* — joined the melody.

The *caeenri-beda* was slowing, then speeding the tempo of the racing Shadow Beasts. The white beast altered its wailing cries to mimic the sounds the Outcasts made on the Horn.

Antibodies charged through the Shadow Beasts wheeling around the villa.

Gyro's heart pounded. He finally understood Yan's plan of action. Was it too late?

The *caeenri-beda* cried seven notes that the rampaging Shadow Beasts imitated.

From the mad chaos of noise came order. Repetition.

Music.

Yan had understood the final lesson of H'Êshra and Ma'h'bri.

Gyro had all the Outcasts sing the same notes being blown on the Horn, the same notes the Shadow Beasts were calling out as they ran.

Antibodies grabbed Shadow Beasts, swung their deadly arms at them, kicked them, injured them — but could not yet defeat them.

If Dulunae could speak its own language, it would now be through the Outcasts, through the *caeenri-beda*, through the Shadow Beasts. The world shouted seven characters now translated into the beauty of music:

C

H

'

N

O

P

S

They sang the one word that could protect them. The word that both recognized its existence and denied its power over them.

"*CH'NOPS.*"

Yan had translated the dread word into a song, a battle cry, a warrior's defense against the most vile attack.

And the Antibodies fell.

It was as if the running circle of Shadow Beasts were a sharp, deadly blade of immense proportion, spinning, creating an impenetrable barrier against the Antibodies. As the Antibodies heard the Horn, the Outcasts, the thousands of Shadow Beasts repeatedly chanting the Seven-Character Word, they froze.

They collapsed on each other. They dropped through the ground into maws of raw earth ready to devour them.

Some continued to fight. Some attacked Shadow Beasts. None reached the villa. The tower. The Font of Knowledge. Not a single Antibody reached the boys and girls known as Outcasts.

Today, the Outcasts were born not as a random scatter of

children from different communities.

Today, they were born of their own place.

The Community of Outcasts.

The attack of the Antibodies seemed relentless, at first. They screamed at the Shadow Beasts, trying to distort the melody of Yan's music. "DIE, BEASTS, DIE!"

They failed.

The battle raged through the night, into the morning, into midday.

Then, there was an overwhelming flash of light in the sky, a final burst of sound that silenced Antibodies, Shadow Beasts, Outcasts, everyone and everything.

All things lay silent and still.

Then a rainbow appeared.

Chapter 32

A rainbow appeared on this new day, curving from a dark, distant land riddled with charred remains, tar pits, death and disease.

The rainbow split the sky, until a multitude of rainbows angled left, right, crosswise, everywhere, filling earth and sky with glorious, colorful light. A cool breeze cleared the air of smoke and stench.

If the being that humans had called CH'NOPS was outraged, it did not show itself on this day. The earth did not tremble, the lands did not crack open, the mountains did not flow with lava. In a land beyond all known time and space, there was only a folding, a cowardly retreat into dark silence, the silence of the conquered.

Antibodies vanished. Some disappeared into the earth, never to be seen again. Some froze like statues. The survivors had been called to retreat, escape, plot and plan again another time. Devise a more sinister attack.

If one listened on this cool, bright day, one might hear a faint, repetitive cry in the distance: "*Een. Een. Een.*" The cries had no power or purpose. At the moment.

The Outcasts lay in the courtyard, protected by sleep. Lynai'seth was the first to stir. She sat up.

"Gyro?"

Gyro moaned. "What hit us?"

"I don't know. But listen."

Gyro, S'yen, Yan, Terra and some of the children rose from sleep and listened.

There was only a soft whisper of wind through surviving trees.

They stood and stepped outside the villa. Xalid wandered off to the Font of Knowledge, which stood battered and broken, but sturdy.

The Shadow Beasts were gone.

The Antibodies had disappeared.

The reality of the situation slowly dawned on everyone. The battle was over.

Rainbows angled from the distant sky, drawing near them.

Terra rubbed her eyes. "Are we still alive?"

"I think so," Gyro said.

"No beasts or monsters coming to get us?"

Gyro smiled. "Not at the moment."

"So we *sang a song* to protect ourselves?"

"That was Yan's idea."

Terra turned to Yan and kissed him. Yan, unaccustomed to contact, buckled to the ground.

Lynai'seth looked into Gyro's eyes. "Thank you."

"No thanks to me. We did this together."

"Thank you," Lynai'seth repeated.

Xalid joined them. "I called for H'Êshra and Ma'h'bri. No answer. They — vanished."

"We'll find them," Gyro said. "First, we need to regroup, treat our wounds, find food and make a new plan."

Lynai'seth touched his arm. "Not yet."

"What?"

"Not yet."

Other Outcasts stepped from the courtyard to join their

leader, Gyro. They all gazed at the approaching rainbows. Oolo helped Kg. Alamine and Amina walked hand-in-hand. Ignis, Ru'an, Mohir'a'qest, Zwyna, Tu'ghee T'an, Lhista T'an and Klanga, with her pet Feelie, walked from the villa to the opening lands beyond the walls.

Gyro pointed to the sky. "There are your 'angles of rainbows,'" he said to Yan.

Yan, still reeling from the splendor of Terra's kiss, realized something fantastic.

I like the here and now.

"Yes," he said to Gyro.

It was the only word spoken.

The Outcasts were silent.

Something approached.

No new menace, no new thought from CH'NOPS.

The 'angles of rainbows' flapped like bright banners in the sky, dancing, tumbling with delight.

Lynai'seth saw. Understood. Smiled. And quietly closed a secret part of her heart. Gyro, unable to contain himself, felt tears welling in his eyes.

Two friends, thought dead, were alive.

Jax was walking with Marina's quarterstaff in hand. Marina was riding side-saddle on the back of a bright white *caeenri-beda.*

As the couple drew near, the Outcasts saw that Marina was carrying a small bundle in her arms.

The rainbows seemed to part in honor of their approach.

Jax smiled his bright, glorious, hopeful Jax smile. He raised his hand over his head and waved to them.

As they approached, it became obvious to everyone.

The Two had found the One.

The One lifted a tiny arm from the bundle in Marina's lap, raised its little hand and pointed skyward.

Old planet Dulunae now spoke in a new language. And its first word was *hope.*

THE OUTCASTS

They are six of the Outcasts, the last survivors of vanished civilizations. At first, they had nothing in common except their determination to survive on a desolate planet.

Gyro—a brave and handsome leader

Lynai'seth—beautiful and mysterious guardian of the children

Yan—mystical and vague, will his visions lead them to happiness or ruin?

Jax—a scout, and a misfit among misfits, he relies on Marina perhaps more than he should

Marina—Jax's co-scout, who wants to be more

Dav'yn—in a world of threat and despair, how does a damaged soul heal?

The Bonds of Friendship Are Their Greatest Strength—and Their Greatest Weakness

But now, with the hope of a HayVen before them, the possibilities are far more great . . . and their enemies much more real.

Antibodies—their skin is as transparent as their will for destruction

The Shadow Beasts—as frightening as they are confusing; on whose side does their loyalty lie?

Book 1:
The Shadow Beasts

Book 2:
The Survivors

Written and illustrated by Gregory Janicke

LOOK FOR
Books 3 and 4
coming to a store near you in 2008!

Gregory Janicke has been writing stories and drawing since he was nine years old. His educational comic strip, "Fizzik Rules," has appeared in *The Baltimore Sun*, *London Free Press* (Canada), *New Straits Times* (Malaysia) and many other newspapers throughout the world. He and his wife, Deborah, currently live in Morocco, where he is creating his next exciting series of stories.